The Critics on Lawrence Block

'Deceptively rambling plot construction which, when you least expect it, snaps shut like a pair of cuffs. As much about alcoholism as it is about crime, dark and fearful passages both, down which Block treads a nimble measure'
Literary Review

'Scudder . . . continues to be one of the most interesting private investigators on the fiction scene . . . Block fleshes out the bare bones of his account with several effective side plots and a great deal of convincingly gritty detail'
The Wall Street Journal

'As enjoyably readable as any in the genre . . . Scudder tells it in the first person . . . which makes the nail-chewing anxiety that Block generates all the more impressive'
Los Angeles Times

'The author is there with the very best . . . The real McCoy with a shocking twist – stylish too' *Observer*

'Bull's-eye dialogue and laser-image description . . . any search for false notes will prove futile; both Block and Scudder's eye for detail is as sharp as ever, and the characters almost real enough to touch'
New York Times Book Review

D1384870

Lawrence Block is a Grandmaster of the Mystery Writers of America, and has won a total of fourteen awards for his fiction, including one Edgar Award and two Shamus Awards for best novels for titles in the Matt Scudder series. He is also the creator of other great characters such as Bernie Rhodenbarr, Evan Tanner and Chip Harrison, and has written dozens of award-winning short stories. Lawrence Block lives in New York City.

IN THE MIDST OF DEATH

A MATT SCUDDER MYSTERY

Lawrence Block

ORION

An Orion Paperback
First published in Great Britain by Orion in 1997
This paperback edition published in 2000 by
Orion Books Ltd,
Orion House, 5 Upper St Martin's Lane,
London WC2H 9EA

A CIP catalogue record for this book
is available from the British Library.

ISBN 0 75283 701 X

Typeset by Deltatype Ltd, Birkenhead, Merseyside
Printed and bound in Great Britain by
Clays Ltd, St Ives plc

For an absent friend

ONE

October is about as good as the city gets. The last of the summer heat is gone and the real bite of cold weather hasn't arrived yet. There had been rain in September, quite a bit of it, but that was past now. The air was a little less polluted than usual, and its temperature made it seem even cleaner than it was.

I stopped at a phone booth on Third Avenue in the Fifties. On the corner an old woman scattered bread crumbs for the pigeons and cooed to them as she fed them. I believe there's a city ordinance against feeding pigeons. We used to cite it in the department when explaining to rookies that there were laws you enforced and laws you forgot about.

I went into the booth. It had been mistaken at least once for a public lavatory, which is par for the course. At least the phone worked. Most of them do these days. Five or six years ago most of the phones in outdoor booths didn't work. So not everything in our world is getting worse. Some things are actually getting better.

I called Portia Carr's number. Her answering machine always picked up on the second ring, so when the phone rang a third time, I figured I'd dialed a wrong number. I'd begun to take it for granted that she would never be home when I called.

Then she answered the phone. 'Yes?'

'Miss Carr?'

'Yes, this is she speaking.' The voice was not pitched quite so low as on the tape of the answering machine, and the Mayfair accent was less noticeable.

'My name is Scudder,' I said. 'I'd like to come over and see you. I'm in the neighborhood and—'

'Terribly sorry,' she cut in. ''Fraid I'm not seeing people anymore. Thank you.'

'I wanted to—'

'Do call someone else.' And she broke the connection.

I found another dime and was set to drop it in the slot and call her again when I changed my mind and put the dime back in my pocket. I walked two blocks downtown and one block east to Second Avenue and Fifty-fourth Street, where I scouted up a lunch counter with a pay phone that was in view of the entrance of her building. I dropped my dime in that phone and dialed her number.

As soon as she came on the line I said, 'My name is Scudder, and I want to talk to you about Jerry Broadfield.'

There was a pause. Then she said, 'Who is this?'

'I told you. My name is Matthew Scudder.'

'You called a few moments ago.'

'Right. You hung up on me.'

'I thought—'

'I know what you thought. I want to talk to you.'

'I'm terribly sorry, don't you know, but I'm not giving interviews.'

'I'm not from the press.'

'Then what *is* your interest, Mr Scudder?'

'You'll find out when you see me. I think you'd better see me, Miss Carr.'

'I think not, actually.'

'I'm not sure you have any choice. I'm in your neighborhood. I'll be at your place in five minutes.'

'No, please.' A pause. 'I've just tumbled out of bed, don't you see? You'll have to give me an hour. Can you give me an hour?'

'If I have to.'

'One hour, then, and you'll come round. You have the address, I suppose?'

I told her I did. I rang off and sat at the counter with a cup of coffee and a roll. I faced the window so that I could keep an eye on her building, and I got my first look at her just as the coffee was getting cool enough to drink. She must have been dressed when we spoke because it only took her seven minutes and change to hit the street.

It wasn't much of an accomplishment to recognize her. The description pinned her all by itself – the fiery mane of dark red hair, the height. And she tied it all together with the regal presence of a lioness.

I stood up and moved toward the door, ready to follow her as soon as I knew where she was going. But she kept walking straight toward the coffee shop, and when she came through the door, I turned away from her and went back to my cup of coffee.

She headed straight for the phone booth.

I suppose I shouldn't have been surprised. Enough telephones are tapped so that everyone who is either criminally or politically active knows to regard *all* phones as tapped and to act accordingly. Important or sensitive calls are not to be made from one's own phone. And this was the nearest public telephone to her building. That's why I had chosen it myself, and it was why she was using it now.

I moved a little closer to the booth, just to satisfy myself that it wouldn't do me any good. I couldn't see the number she was dialing, and I couldn't hear a thing. Once I'd established this, I paid for my roll and coffee and left.

I crossed the street and walked over to her building. I was taking a chance. If she finished her call and hopped into a cab I would lose her, and I didn't want to lose her now. Not after all the time it had taken me to find her. I wanted to know who she was calling now, and if she went someplace I wanted to know where and why.

But I didn't think she was going to grab a taxi. She hadn't even been carrying a purse, and if she wanted to go somewhere, she would probably want to come back for her bag first and throw some clothes in a suitcase. And she had set things up with me to give herself an hour's leeway.

So I went to her building and found a little white-haired guy on the door. He had guileless blue eyes and a rash of broken capillaries on his cheekbones. He looked as though he took a lot of pride in his uniform.

'Carr,' I said.

'Just left a minute ago. You just missed her, couldn't have been more than a minute.'

'I know.' I took out my wallet and flipped it open quickly. There was nothing there for him to see, not even a junior G-man's badge, but it didn't matter. It's the moves that do it, that and looking like a cop in the first place. He got a quick flash of leather and was suitably impressed. It would have been bad form for him to demand a closer look.

'What apartment?'

'I sure hope you don't get me in trouble.'

'Not if you play it by the book. Which apartment is she in?'

'Four G.'

'Give me your passkey, huh?'

'I'm not supposed to do that.'

'Uh-huh. You want to go downtown and talk about it?'

He didn't. What he wanted was for me to go someplace and die, but he didn't say so. He turned over his passkey.

'She'll be back in a couple of minutes. You wouldn't want to tell her I'm upstairs.'

'I don't like this.'

'You don't have to.'

'She's a nice lady, always been nice to me.'

'Generous at Christmastime, huh?'

'She's a very pleasant person,' he said.

'I'm sure you've got a swell relationship. But tip her off and I'll know about it, and I won't be happy. You follow me?'

'I'm not going to say anything.'

'And you'll get your key back. Don't worry about it.'

'That's the least of it,' he said.

I took the elevator to the fourth floor. The G apartment faced the street, and I sat at her window and watched the entrance of the coffee shop. I couldn't tell from that angle whether there was anyone in the phone booth or not, so she could have left already, could have

5

ducked around the corner and into a cab, but I didn't think so. I sat there in a chair and I waited, and after about ten minutes she came out of the coffee shop and stood on the corner, long and tall and striking.

And evidently uncertain. She just stood there for a long moment, and I could read the indecision in her mind. She could have gone in almost any direction. But after a moment she turned decisively and began walking back toward me. I let out a breath I hadn't realized I'd been holding and settled down to wait for her.

When I heard her key in the lock, I moved from the window and flattened out against the wall. She opened the door, closed it behind her, and shot the bolt. She was doing a very efficient job of locking the door but I was already inside it.

She took off a pale blue trenchcoat and hung it in the front closet. Under it she'd been wearing a knee-length plaid skirt and a tailored yellow blouse with a button-down collar. She had very long legs and a powerful, athletic body.

She turned again, and her eyes did not quite reach the spot where I was standing, and I said, 'Hello, Portia.'

The scream didn't get out. She stopped it by clapping her own hand over her mouth. She stood very still for a moment, her body balanced on the tips of her toes, and then she willed her hand to drop from her mouth as she settled back down on her heels. She took a deep breath and made herself hang onto it. Her coloring was very fair to begin with, but now her face looked bleached. She put her hand over her heart. The gesture looked

6

theatrical, insincere. As if she recognized this, she lowered her hand again and breathed deeply several times, in and out, in and out.

'Your name is—'

'Scudder.'

'You called before.'

'Yes.'

'You promised to give me an hour.'

'My watch has been running fast lately.'

'Has it indeed.' She took another very deep breath and let it out slowly. She closed her eyes. I moved out from my post against the wall and stood in the middle of the room within a few steps of her. She didn't look like the sort of person who faints easily, and if she were she probably would have done it already, but she was still very pale and if she was going to flop I wanted a fair shot at catching her on the way down. But the color began to seep back into her face and she opened her eyes.

'I need something to drink,' she announced. 'Will you have something?'

'No, thanks.'

'So I drink alone.' She went to the kitchen. I followed close enough to keep her in sight. She took a fifth of Scotch and a split of club soda from the refrigerator and poured about three ounces of each into a glass. 'No ice,' she said. 'I don't fancy the cubes bumping up against my teeth. But I've got into the habit of taking my drinks chilled. Rooms are kept warmer here, you know, so that room-temperature drinks won't do at all. You're sure you won't join me?'

'Not right now.'

'Cheers, then.' She got rid of the drink in one very

long swallow. I watched the muscles work in her throat. A long, lovely neck. She had that perfect English skin and it took a lot of it to cover her. I'm about six feet tall and she was at least my height and maybe a little taller. I pictured her with Jerry Broadfield, who had about four inches on her and could match her with presence of his own. They must have made a striking couple.

She drew another breath, shuddered, and put the empty glass in the sink. I asked her if she was all right.

'Oh, just peachy,' she said. Her eyes were a very pale blue verging on gray, her mouth full but bloodless. I stepped aside and she walked past me into the living room. Her hips just barely brushed me as she passed. That was just about enough. It wouldn't take much more than that, not with her.

She sat on a slate-blue sofa and took a small cigar from a teak box that rested on a clear Plexiglas end table. She lit the cigar with a wooden match, then gestured at the box for me to help myself. I told her I didn't smoke.

'I switched to these because one doesn't inhale them,' she said. 'So I inhale them just the same and of course they are stronger than cigarettes. How did you get in here?'

I held up the key.

'Timmie gave you that?'

'He didn't want to. I didn't give him much choice. He says you've always been nice to him.'

'I tip him enough, the silly little fuck. You gave me a fright, you know. I don't know what you want or why you're here. Or who you are, for that matter. I seem to have forgotten your name already.' I supplied it.

'Matthew,' she said. 'I do not know why you are here, Matthew.'

'Who did you phone from the coffee shop?'

'You were there? I didn't notice you.'

'Who did you call?'

She bought time by puffing on her cigar. Her eyes grew thoughtful. 'I don't think I'm going to tell you,' she said at length.

'Why are you pressing charges against Jerry Broadfield?'

'For extortion.'

'Why, Miss Carr?'

'You called me Portia before. Or was that just for shock value? The peelers always call you by your first name. That's to show their contempt for you, it's supposed to give them some sort of psychological advantage, isn't it?' She pointed at me with her cigar. 'You. You're not a policeman, are you?'

'No.'

'But there's something about you.'

'I used to be a cop.'

'Ah.' She nodded, satisfied. 'And you knew Jerry when you were a policeman?'

'I didn't know him then.'

'But you know him now.'

'That's right.'

'And you're a friend of his? No, that's not possible. Jerry doesn't have friends, does he?'

'Doesn't he?'

'Hardly. You'd know that if you knew him well.'

'I don't know him well.'

'I wonder if anyone does.' Another puff on the cigar,

a careful flicking of ash into a sculptured glass ashtray. 'Jerry Broadfield has acquaintances. Any number of acquaintances. But I doubt he has a friend in the world.'

'You're certainly not his friend.'

'I never said I was.'

'Why charge him with extortion?'

'Because the charge is true.' She managed a small smile. 'He insisted I give him money. A hundred dollars a week or he would make trouble for me. Prostitutes are vulnerable creatures, you know. And a hundred dollars a week isn't so terribly much when you consider the enormous sums men are willing to pay to go to bed with one.' She gestured with her hands, indicating her body. 'So I paid him,' she said. 'The money he asked for, and I made myself available to him sexually.'

'For how long?'

'About an hour at a time, generally. Why?'

'For how long had you been paying him?'

'Oh, I don't know. About a year, I suppose.'

'And you've been in this country how long?'

'Just over three years.'

'And you don't want to go back, do you?' I got to my feet, walked over to the couch. 'That's probably how they set the hook,' I said. 'Play the game their way or they'll get you deported as an undesirable alien. Is that how they pitched you?'

'What a phrase. An undesirable alien.'

'Is that what they—'

'Most people consider me a highly desirable alien.' The cold eyes challenged me. 'I don't suppose you have an opinion on the subject?'

She was getting to me, and it bothered the hell out of

me. I didn't much like her, so why should she be getting to me? I remembered something Elaine Mardell had said to the effect that a large portion of Portia Carr's client list consisted of masochists. I have never really understood what gets a masochist off, but a few minutes in her presence was enough to make me realize that a masochist would find this particular woman a perfect component for his fantasies. And, in a somewhat different way, she fit nicely into my own.

We went around and around for a while. She kept insisting that Broadfield had really been extorting cash from her, and I kept trying to get past that to the person who had induced her to do the job on him. We weren't getting anywhere – that is, *I* wasn't getting anywhere, and she didn't have anyplace to get to.

So I said, 'Look, when you come right down to it, it doesn't matter at all. It doesn't matter whether he was getting money from you, and it doesn't matter who got you to press charges against him.'

'Then why are you here, angel? Just for love?'

'What matters is what it'll take to get you to drop the charges.'

'What's the hurry?' She smiled. 'Jerry hasn't even been arrested yet, has he?'

'You're not going to take it all the way to the courtroom,' I went on. 'You'd need proof to get an indictment, and if you had any it would have come out by now. So this is just a smear, but it's an awkward smear for him and he'd like to wipe it up. What does it take to get the charges dropped?'

'Jerry must know that.'

'Oh?'

'All he has to do is stop doing what he's been doing.'

'You mean with Prejanian.'

'Do I?' She had finished her cigar, and now she took another from the teak box. But she didn't light it, just played with it. 'Maybe I don't mean anything. But look at the record. That's an Americanism I rather like. Let us look at the record. For all these years Jerry has been doing nicely as a policeman. He has his charming little house in Forest Hills and his charming wife and his charming children. Have you met his wife and children?'

'No.'

'Neither have I, but I've seen their pictures. American men are extraordinary. First they show one pictures of their wives and children, and then they want to go to bed. Are you married?'

'Not anymore.'

'Did you play around when you were?'

'Now and then.'

'But you didn't show pictures around, did you?' I shook my head. 'Somehow I didn't think so.' She returned the cigar to the box, straightened up, yawned. 'He had all that, at any rate, and then he went to this Special Prosecutor with this long story about police corruption, and he began giving interviews to the newspapers, and he took a leave of absence from the police force, and all of a sudden he's in trouble and accused of shaking down a poor little whore for a hundred dollars a week. It makes you wonder, doesn't it?'

'That's what he has to do? Drop Prejanian and you'll drop the charges?'

'I didn't come right out and say that, did I? And

anyway, he must have known that without your digging around. I mean, it's rather obvious, wouldn't you say?'

We went around a little more and didn't accomplish a thing. I don't know what I'd hoped to accomplish or why I had taken five hundred dollars from Broadfield in the first place. Someone had Portia Carr intimidated a lot more seriously than I was likely to manage, for all my cleverness in sneaking into her apartment. In the meantime we were talking pointlessly, and we were both aware of the pointlessness of it.

'This is silly,' she said at one point. 'I am going to have another drink. Will you join me?'

I wanted a drink badly. 'I'll pass.' I said.

She brushed me on the way to the kitchen. I got a strong whiff of a perfume I didn't recognize. I decided I would know it the next time I smelled it. She came back with a drink in her hand and sat on the couch again. 'Silly,' she said again. 'Why don't you come sit next to me and we will talk of something else. Or of nothing at all.'

'You could be in trouble, Portia.'

Her face showed alarm. 'You mustn't say that.'

'You're putting yourself right in the middle. You're a big strong girl, but you might not turn out to be as strong as you think you are.'

'Are you threatening me? No, it's not a threat, is it?'

I shook my head. 'You don't have to worry about me. But you've got enough to worry about without me.'

Her eyes dropped. 'I'm so tired of being strong,' she said. 'I'm good at it, you know.'

'I'm sure you are.'

'But it's tiring.'

'Maybe I could help you.'

'I don't think anyone can.'

'Oh?'

She studied me briefly, then dropped her eyes. She stood and crossed the room to the window. I could have walked along behind her. There was something in her stance that suggested she expected me to. But I stayed where I was.

She said, 'There's something there, isn't there?'

'Yes.'

'But it's just no good at the moment. The timing's all wrong.' She was looking out the window. 'Right now neither of us can do the other any good at all.'

I didn't say anything.

'You'd better go now.'

'All right.'

'It's so beautiful outside. The sun, the freshness of the air.' She turned to look at me. 'Do you like this time of year?'

'Yes. Very much.'

'It's my favorite, I think. October, November, the best time of the year. But also the saddest, wouldn't you say?'

'Sad? Why?'

'Oh, very sad,' she said. 'Because winter is coming.'

TWO

On my way out I left the passkey with the doorman. He didn't seem any happier now, even though he was getting to see me leave this time. I went over to Johnny Joyce's on Second and sat in a booth. Most of the lunch crowd was gone. The ones who remained were one or two martinis over the line now and probably wouldn't make it back to their offices at all. I had a hamburger and a bottle of Harp, then drank a couple shots of bourbon with my coffee.

I tried Broadfield's number. It rang for a while and no one answered it. I went back to my booth and had another bourbon and thought about some things. There were questions I couldn't seem to answer. Why had I passed up Portia Carr's offer of a drink when I wanted a drink so badly? And why (if it wasn't another version of the same question) had I passed up Portia Carr herself?

I did some more thinking on West Forty-ninth Street, in the actors' chapel at St Malachy's. The chapel is below street level, a large understated room which provides a measure of peace and quiet that is otherwise hard to come by in the heart of the Broadway theater district. I took an aisle seat and let my mind wander.

An actress I used to know a long time ago once told me that she came to St Malachy's every day when she wasn't working. '*I wonder if it matters that I'm not a*

Catholic, Matt. I don't think so. I say my little prayer and I light my little candle and I pray for work. I wonder whether or not it helps. Do you suppose it's okay to ask God for a decent part?'

I must have sat there for close to an hour, running different things through my mind. On the way out I put a couple of bucks in the poor box and lit a few candles. I didn't say any prayers.

I spent most of the evening in Polly's Cage, across the street from my hotel. Chuck was behind the bar and he was in an expansive mood, so much so that the house was buying every other round. I had reached my client late in the afternoon and had given him a brief rundown on my meeting with Carr. He'd asked me where I was going to go from there, and I'd said I would have to work it out and that I'd get in touch when I had something he ought to know. Nothing in that category came up that night, so I didn't have to call him. Nor did I have any reason to call anyone else. I'd picked up a phone message at my hotel: Anita had called and wanted me to call her, but it was not the sort of night on which I wanted to talk to an ex-wife. I stayed at Polly's and emptied my glass every time Chuck filled it up.

Around eleven-thirty a couple of kids came in and started playing nothing but country and western on the jukebox. I can usually stomach that as well as anything else, but for some reason or other it wasn't what I wanted to hear just then. I settled my tab and went around the corner to Armstrong's, where Don had the radio set to WNCN. They were playing Mozart, and the crowd was so thin you could actually hear the music.

'They sold the station,' Don said. 'The new owners are switching to a pop-rock format. Another rock station is just what the city needs.'

'Things always deteriorate.'

'I can't argue the point. There's a protest movement to force them to continue a classical music policy. I don't suppose it'll do any good, do you?'

I shook my head. 'Nothing ever does any good.'

'Well, you're in a beautiful mood tonight. I'm glad you decided to spread sweetness and light here instead of staying cooped up in your room.'

I poured bourbon into my coffee and gave it a stir. I *was* in a foul mood and I couldn't figure out exactly why. It is bad enough when you know what it is that is bothering you. When the demons plaguing you are invisible, it is that much more difficult to contend with them.

It was a strange dream.

I don't dream much. Alcohol has this effect of making you sleep at a deeper level, below the plane on which dreams occur. I am told that d.t.'s represent the psyche's insistence upon having its chance to dream; unable to dream while asleep, one has one's dreams upon awakening. But I haven't had d.t.'s yet and am grateful for my generally dreamless sleep. There was a time when this, in and of itself, was a sufficient argument for drinking.

But that night I dreamed, and the dream struck me as strange. She was in it. Portia, with her size and her striking beauty and her deep voice and her good English accent. And we were sitting and talking, she and I, but not in her apartment. We were in a police station. I don't know what precinct it might have been but remember that I felt at home there, so perhaps it was a place where I had been stationed once. There were uniformed cops walking around, and citizens filing complaints, and all of the extras playing the same roles in my dream that they play in similar scenes in cops-and-robbers movies.

And we were in the midst of all this, Portia and I, and we were naked. We were going to make love, but we had to establish something first through conversation. I don't recall what it was that had to be established, but our conversation went on and on, getting ever more abstract, and we got no closer to the bedroom, and then the telephone rang and Portia reached out and answered it in the voice of her answering machine.

Except that it went on ringing.

My phone, of course. I had incorporated its ring into my dream. If it hadn't awakened me with its ringing I'm sure I would ultimately have forgotten the dream entirely. Instead I shook myself awake while shaking off the vestiges of the dream. I fumbled for the phone and got the receiver to my ear.

'Hello?'

'Matt, I'm sorry as hell if I woke you. I—'

'Who is this?'

'Jerry. Jerry Broadfield.'

I usually put my watch on the bedside table when I

turn in. I groped around for it now but couldn't find it. I said, 'Broadfield?'

'I guess you were sleeping. Look, Matt—'

'What time is it?'

'A few minutes after six. I just—'

'Christ!'

'Matt, are you awake?'

'Yeah, damn it, I'm awake. Christ. I said call me, but I didn't say call me in the middle of the night.'

'Look, it's an emergency. Will you just let me talk?' For the first time I was aware of the band of tension in his voice. It must have been there all along, but I hadn't noticed it before. 'I'm sorry I woke you,' he was saying, 'but I finally got a chance to make a phone call and I don't know how long they'll let me stay on. Just let me talk for a minute.'

'Where the hell are you?'

'Men's House of Detention.'

'The Tombs?'

'That's right, the Tombs.' He was talking quickly now, as if to get it all out before I could interrupt again. 'They were waiting for me. At the apartment. Barrow Street, they were waiting for me. I got back there about two-thirty and they were waiting for me and this is the first chance I've had to get to a phone. As soon as I finish with you I'm calling a lawyer. But I'm going to need more than a lawyer, Matt. They got the deck stacked too good for anybody to straighten things out in front of a jury. They got me by the balls.'

'What are you talking about?'

'Portia.'

'What about her?'

'Somebody killed her last night. Strangled her or something, dumped her in my apartment, then tipped the cops. I don't know all the details. They booked me for it. Matt, I didn't do it.'

I didn't say anything.

His voice rose, verging on hysteria. 'I didn't do it. Why would I kill the cunt? And leave her in my apartment? It doesn't make any sense, Matt, but it doesn't have to make any sense because the whole fucking thing is a frame and they can make it stick. Matt, they're gonna make it stick!'

'Easy, Broadfield.'

Silence. I pictured him gritting his teeth, forcing his emotions back under control like an animal trainer cracking his whip at a cageful of lions and tigers. 'Right,' he said, the voice crisp again. 'I'm exhausted and it's starting to get to me. Matt, I'm going to need help on this one. From you, Matt. I can pay you whatever you ask.'

I told him to hang on for a minute. I had been asleep for maybe three hours and I was finally becoming awake enough to realize just how rotten I felt. I put the phone down and went into the bathroom and splashed cold water on my face. I was careful not to look in the mirror because I had a fair idea what the face that glowered back at me might look like. There was about an inch of bourbon left in the quart on my dresser. I took a slug of it straight from the bottle, shuddered, sat down on the bed again and picked up the phone.

I asked him if he'd been booked.

'Just now. For homicide. Once they booked me they couldn't keep me away from a phone any longer. You know what they did? They informed me of my rights when they arrested me. That whole speech, *Miranda-Escobedo*, how many times do you figure I read out that goddam little set piece to some fucking crook? And they had to read it out to me word for word.'

'You've got a lawyer to call?'

'Yeah. Guy who's supposed to be good, but there's no way he can do it all.'

'Well, I don't know what I can do for you.'

'Can you come down here? Not now, I can't see anybody right now. Hang on a minute.' He must have turned away from the phone, but I could hear him asking someone when he could have visitors. 'Ten o'clock,' he told me. 'Could you get here between ten and noon?'

'I suppose so.'

'I got a lot of things to tell you, Matt, but I can't do it over the phone.'

I told him I'd see him sometime after ten. I cradled the phone and tapped the bourbon bottle for another small taste. My head ached dully and I suspected that bourbon was probably not the best thing in the world for it, but I couldn't think of anything better. I got back into bed and pulled the blankets over me. I needed sleep and knew I wasn't going to get any, but at least I could stay horizontal for another hour or two and get a little rest.

Then I remembered the dream I'd been yanked out of by his call. I remembered it, got a clean, vivid flash of it, and started to shake.

THREE

It had started two days earlier, on a crisply cold Tuesday afternoon. I was getting the day started at Armstrong's, doing my usual balancing act with coffee and bourbon, coffee to speed things up and bourbon to slow them down. I was reading the *Post* and I was sufficiently involved in what I was reading so that I didn't even notice when he pulled back the chair opposite mine and dropped into it. Then he cleared his throat and I looked up at him.

He was a little guy with a lot of curly black hair. His cheeks were sunken, his forehead very prominent. He wore a goatee but kept his upper lip clean shaven. His eyes, magnified by thick glasses, were dark brown and highly animated.

He said, 'Busy, Matt?'

'Not really.'

'I wanted to talk to you for a minute.'

'Sure.'

I knew him, but not terribly well. His name was Douglas Fuhrmann and he was a regular at Armstrong's. He didn't drink a hell of a lot, but he was apt to drop in four or five times a week, sometimes with a girlfriend, sometimes on his own. He'd generally nurse a beer and talk for a while about sports or politics or whatever conversational topic was on the agenda. He was a writer, as I understood it, although I didn't recall having heard him discuss his work. But he evidently did well enough so that he didn't have to hold a job.

I asked what was on his mind.

'A fellow I know wants to see you, Matt.'

'Oh?'

'I think he'd like to hire you.'

'Bring him around.'

'That's not possible.'

'Oh?'

He started to say something, then stopped because Trina was on her way to find out what he wanted to drink. He ordered a beer and we sat there awkwardly while she went for the beer, brought it, and went away again.

Then he said, 'It's complicated. He can't be seen in public. He's, well, hiding out.'

'Who is he?'

'This is confidential.' I gave him a look. 'Well, all right. If that's today's *Post*, maybe you read about him. You would have read about him anyway, he's been all over the papers the past few weeks.'

'What's his name?'

'Jerry Broadfield.'

'Is that right.'

'He's very hot right now,' Fuhrmann said. 'Ever since the English girl filed charges against him he's been hiding out. But he can't hide forever.'

'Where's he hiding?'

'An apartment he has. He wants you to see him there.'

'Where is it?'

'The Village.'

I picked up my cup of coffee and looked into it as if it was going to tell me something. 'Why me?' I said. 'What does he think I can do for him? I don't get it.'

'He wants me to take you there,' Fuhrmann said. 'There's some money in it for you, Matt. How about it?'

We took a cab down Ninth Avenue and wound up on Barrow Street near Bedford. I let Fuhrmann pay for the cab. We went into the vestibule of a five-storey walk-up. More than half the doorbells lacked identifying labels. Either the building was being vacated preparatory to demolition or Broadfield's fellow tenants shared his desire for anonymity. Fuhrmann rang one of the unlabeled bells, pushed the button three times, waited, pushed it once, then pushed it three times again.

'It's a code,' he said.

'One if by land and two if by sea.'

'Huh?'

'Forget it.'

There was a buzz and he shoved the door open. 'You go on up,' he said. 'The D apartment on the third floor.'

'You're not coming?'

'He wants to see you alone.'

I was halfway up one flight before it occurred to me that this was a cute way to set me up for something. Fuhrmann had taken himself out of the picture, and there was no way of knowing what I'd find in apartment 3D. But there was also no one I could think of with a particularly good reason for wanting to do me substantial harm. I stopped halfway up the stairs to think it over, my curiosity fighting a successful battle against my more sensible desire to turn around and go home and stay out of it. I walked on up to the third floor and knocked three-one-three on the appropriate door. It opened almost before I'd finished knocking.

He looked just like his photographs. He'd been all over the papers for the past few weeks, ever since he'd begun cooperating with Abner Prejanian's investigation of corruption in the New York Police Department. But the news photos didn't give you the sense of height. He stood six-four easy and was built to scale, broad in the shoulders, massive in the chest. He was starting to thicken in the gut as well; he was in his early thirties now, and in another ten years he'd add on another forty or fifty pounds and he'd need every inch of his height to carry it well.

If he lived another ten years.

He said, 'Where's Doug?'

'He left me at the door. Said you wanted to see me alone.'

'Yeah, but the knock, I thought it was him.'

'I cracked the code.'

'Huh? Oh.' He grinned suddenly, and it really did light up the room. He had a lot of teeth and he let me look at them, but the grin did more than that. It brightened his whole face. 'So you're Matt Scudder,' he said. 'Come on in, Matt. It's not much but it's better than a jail cell.'

'Can they put you in jail?'

'They can try. They're damn well trying.'

'What have they got on you?'

'They've got a crazy English cunt that somebody's

25

got a hold on. How much do you know about what's going on?'

'Just what I read in the papers.'

And I hadn't paid all that much attention to the papers. So I knew his name was Jerome Broadfield and he was a cop. He'd been on the force a dozen years. Six or seven years ago he made plainclothes, and a couple of years after that he made detective third, which was where he had stayed. Then a matter of weeks ago he threw his shield in a drawer and started helping Prejanian stand the NYPD on its ear.

I stood around while he bolted the door. I was taking the measure of the place. It looked as though the landlord had leased it furnished, and nothing about the apartment held any clues to the nature of its tenant.

'The papers,' he said. 'Well, they're close. They say Portia Carr was a whore. Well, they're right about that. They say I knew her. That's true, too.'

'And they say you were shaking her down.'

'Wrong. They say she *says* I was shaking her down.'

'Were you?'

'No. Here, sit down, Matt. Make yourself comfortable. How about a drink, huh?'

'All right.'

'I got scotch, I got vodka, I got bourbon, and I think there's a little brandy.'

'Bourbon's good.'

'Rocks? Soda?'

'Just straight.'

He made drinks. Neat bourbon for me, a long scotch and soda for himself. I sat on a tufted greenprint couch and he sat on a matching club chair. I sipped bourbon.

26

He got a pack of Winstons out of the breast pocket of his suit jacket and offered me one. I shook my head and he lit it for himself. The lighter he used was a Dunhill, either gold-plated or solid gold. The suit looked custom-made, and the shirt was definitely made to measure, with his monogram gracing the breast pocket.

We looked at each other over our drinks. He had a large, square-jawed face, prominent brows over blue eyes, one of the eyebrows bisected by an old scar. His hair was sand-colored and just a shade too short to be aggressively fashionable. The face looked open and honest, but after I'd been looking at it for a while I decided it was just a pose. He knew how to use his face to his advantage.

He watched the smoke rise from his cigarette as if it had something to tell him. He said, 'The newspapers make me look pretty bad, don't they? Smart-ass cop finks on the whole department, and then it turns out he's scoring off some poor little hooker. Hell, you were on the force. How many years was it?'

'Around fifteen.'

'So you know about newspapers. The press doesn't necessarily get everything right. They're in business to sell papers.'

'So?'

'So reading the papers you got to get one of two impressions of me. Either I'm a crook who let the Special Prosecutor's office get some kind of hammer-lock on me or else I'm some kind of a nut.'

'Which is right?'

He flashed a grin. 'Neither. Christ, I been on the force going on thirteen years. I didn't just figure out yesterday that a couple of guys are maybe taking a dollar now and then. And nobody had anything on me at all. They been issuing denials out of Prejanian's office left and right. They said all along I was cooperating voluntarily, that I had come to them unasked, the whole number. Look, Matt, they're human. If they managed to set me up and turn me around on their own they'd be bragging about it, not denying it. But they're as much as saying I walked in and handed it all to them on a platter.'

'So?'

'So it's the truth. That's all.'

Did he think I was a priest? I didn't care whether he was a nut or a crook or both or neither. I didn't want to hear his confession. He had had me brought here, presumably for a purpose, and now he was justifying himself to me.

No man has to justify himself to me. I have trouble enough justifying myself to myself.

'Matt, I got a problem.'

'You said they don't have anything on you.'

'This Portia Carr. She's saying I was shaking her down. I demanded a hundred a week or I was going to bust her.'

'But it's not true.'

'No, it's not.'

'So she can't prove it.'

'No. She can't prove shit.'

'Then what's the problem?'

'She also says I was fucking her.'

'Oh.'

'Yeah. I don't know if she can prove that part of it,

but hell, it's the truth. It was no big deal, you know. I was never a saint. Now it's all over the papers and there's this extortion bullshit, and all of a sudden I don't know whether I'm coming or going. My marriage is a little shaky to begin with, and all my wife needs is stories for her friends and family to read about how I'm shacking up with this English cunt. You married, Matt?'

'I used to be.'

'Divorced? Any kids?'

'Two boys.'

'I got two girls and a boy.' He sipped his drink, ducked ash from his cigarette. 'I don't know, maybe you like being divorced. I don't want any part of it. And the extortion charge, that's breaking my balls. I'm scared to leave this fucking apartment.'

'Whose place is it? I always thought Fuhrmann lived in my neighborhood.'

'He's in the West Fifties. That your neighborhood?' I nodded. 'Well, this place is mine, Matt. I've had it a little over a year. I got the house out in Forest Hills and I figured it'd be nice to have a place in town in case I needed one.'

'Who knows about this place?'

'Nobody.' He leaned over, stubbed out his cigarette. 'There's a story they tell about these politicians,' he said. 'This one guy, the polls show he's in trouble, his opponent is wiping the floor with him. So his campaign manager says, "Okay, what we'll do, we'll spread a story about him. We'll tell everybody he fucks pigs." So the candidate asks if it's true, and the campaign manager

29

says it's not. "So we'll let him deny it," he says. "We'll let him deny it."'

'I follow you.'

'Throw enough mud and some of it sticks. Some fucking cop is leaning on Portia, that's what's happening. He wants me to stop working with Prejanian and in return she'll drop the charges. That's what it's all about.'

'Do you know who's doing it?'

'No. But I can't break it off with Abner. And I want those charges dropped. They can't do anything to me in court, but that's not the point. Even without going to court they'll have a departmental investigation. Except they won't be investigating a damn thing because they already know what conclusion they want to come up with. They'll suspend me immediately and they'll wind up kicking me out of the department.'

'I thought you resigned.'

He shook his head. 'Why would I resign, for Christ's sake? I got better than twelve years, close to thirteen. Why would I quit now? I took a leave of absence when I first decided to get in touch with Prejanian. You can't be on active duty and play ball with the Special Prosecutor at the same time. The department would have too many openings to shaft you. But I never even thought about resigning. When this is over I expect to be back on the force.'

I looked at him. If he really meant that last sentence, then he was a whole lot stupider than he looked or acted. I didn't know his angle in helping Prejanian, but I knew he was finished for life as far as the police department was concerned. He had turned himself into an untouchable and he would wear the caste mark as long as he lived. It didn't matter whether the investigation shook up the department or not. It didn't matter who was forced to put in for early retirement or who went to slam. None of that mattered. Every cop on the force, clean or dirty, straight or bent, would mark Jerome Broadfield lousy for the rest of his life.

And he had to know it. He'd been carrying a badge for over twelve years.

I said, 'I don't see where I come in.'

'Freshen that drink for you, Matt?'

'No, I'm fine. Where *do* I come in, Broadfield?'

He cocked his head, narrowed his eyes. 'Simple,' he said. 'You used to be a cop so you know the moves. And you're a private detective now so you can operate freely. And—'

'I'm not a private detective.'

'That's what I heard.'

'Detectives take complicated examinations to get their licenses. They charge fees and keep records and file income tax returns. I don't do any of those things. Sometimes I'll do certain things for certain friends. As a favor. They sometimes give me money. As a favor.'

He cocked his head again, then nodded thoughtfully, as if to say that he had known there was a gimmick and that he was happy to know what the gimmick was. Because everybody had an angle and this was mine and he was sharp enough to appreciate it. The boy liked angles.

If he liked angles, what the hell was he doing with Abner Prejanian?

'Well,' he said. 'Detective or not, you could do me a

favor. You could see Portia and find out just how tied up in this she wants to be. You could see what kind of a hold they got on her and how we could maybe break the hold. One big thing would be finding out who it is that's got her filing charges. If we knew the bastard's name, we could figure out how to deal with him.'

He went on this way, but I wasn't paying too much attention. When he slowed to take a breath I said, 'They want you to cool it with Prejanian. Get out of town, stop cooperating, something like that.'

'That has to be what they want.'

'So why don't you?'

He stared at me. 'You got to be kidding.'

'Why did you tie up with Prejanian in the first place?'

'That's my business, Matt, don't you think? I'm hiring you to do something for me.' Maybe the words sounded a little sharp to him. He tried softening them with a smile. 'The hell, Matt, it's not like you have to know my date of birth and the amount of change in my pocket in order to help me out. Right?'

'Prejanian didn't have a thing on you. You just walked in on your own and told him you had information that could shake up the whole department.'

'That's right.'

'And it's not as though you spent the last twelve years wearing blinders. You're not a choirboy.'

'Me?' A big, toothy grin. 'Not hardly, Matt.'

'Then I don't get it. Where's your angle?'

'Do I have to have an angle?'

'You never walked down the street without one.'

He thought about it and decided not to resent the

line. Instead he chuckled. 'And do you have to know my angle, Matt?'

'Uh-huh.'

He sipped his drink and thought it over. I was almost hoping he would tell me to fuck off. I wanted to go away and forget about him. He was a man I'd never like involved in something I couldn't understand. I really didn't want to get mixed up in any of his problems.

Then he said, 'You of all people should understand.'

I didn't say anything.

'You were on the force fifteen years, Matt. Right? And you got the promotions, you did pretty good, so you musta known the score. You had to be a guy who played the game. Am I right?'

'Keep talking.'

'So you got fifteen years in and five to go for the meal ticket and you pack it in. Puts you in the same boat as me, doesn't it? You reach a point where you can't hack it anymore. The corruption, the shake-downs, the payoffs. It gets to you. Your case, you just pack it in and get out of it. I can respect that. Believe me, I can respect it. I considered it myself, but then I decided it wasn't enough for me, the approach wasn't right for me, I couldn't just walk away from something I had twelve years in.'

'Going on thirteen.'

'Huh?'

'Nothing. You were saying?'

'I was saying I couldn't just turn my back and walk away. I had to do something to make it better. Not all the way better, but maybe just a little bit better, and that means some heads will have to roll, and I'm sorry about that, but it has to be that way.' A wide grin, sudden and alarming now on this face that has been so preoccupied with the business of being sincere. 'Look, Matt, I'm not some fucking Christer. I'm an angle guy, you called me on that and it's true. I know things that Abner has trouble believing. A guy who's absolutely straight, he's never going to hear these things because the wise guys'll dummy up when he walks into the room. But a guy like me gets a chance to hear everything.' He leaned forward. 'I'll tell you something. Maybe you don't know it, maybe it wasn't quite this bad yet when you were carrying a badge. But this whole fucking city is for sale. You can buy the police force all across the board. Straight on up to Murder One.'

'I never heard that.' Which wasn't quite true. I'd heard it. I'd just never believed it.

'Not every cop, Matt. Not hardly. But I know two cases — that's two I know for a fact — where guys got caught with their cocks on the block for homicide and they bought theirselves out from under. And narcotics, fuck, I don't have to tell you about narcotics. That's an open secret. Every heavy dealer keeps a couple of thou in a special pocket. He won't go out on the street without it. That's called walkaway money — you lay it on the cop who busts you and he lets you walk away.'

Was it always that way? It seemed to me that it wasn't. There were always cops who took, some who took a little and some who took a lot, some who didn't say no when easy money came their way, others who actually went out and hustled for it. But there were also things that nobody ever did. Nobody took murder money, and nobody took narcotics money.

But things do change.

'So you just got sick of it,' I said.

'That's right. And you're the last person I should have to explain it to.'

'I didn't leave the force because of corruption.'

'Oh? My mistake.'

I stood up and walked over to where he'd left the bourbon bottle. I freshened my drink and drank off half of it. Still on my feet I said, 'Corruption never bothered me much. It put a lot of food on my family's table.' I was talking as much to myself as to Broadfield. He didn't really care why I left the force any more than I cared whether he knew the right reason or not. 'I took what came my way. I didn't walk around with my hand out and I never let a man buy his way out of something I considered a serious crime, but there was never a week when we lived on what the city paid me.' I drained my glass. 'You take plenty. The city didn't buy that suit.'

'No question.' The grin again. I didn't like that grin much. 'I took plenty, Matt. No argument. But we all have certain lines we draw, right? Why did you quit, anyway?'

'I didn't like the hours.'

'Seriously.'

'That's serious enough.'

It was as much as I felt like telling him. For all I knew he already had the whole story, or whatever the back-fence version of it sounded like these days.

What happened was simple enough. A few years

back I was having a few drinks in a bar in Washington Heights. I was off duty and entitled to drink if I felt like it, and the bar was one where cops could drink on the arm, which may have constituted police corruption but which had never given me a sleepless night.

Then a couple of punks held up the place and shot the bartender dead on their way out. I chased them down the street and emptied my service revolver at them, and I killed one of the bastards and crippled the other, but one bullet didn't go where it was supposed to. It ricocheted off something or other and into the eye of a seven-year-old girl named Estrellita Rivera, and on through the eye and into the brain, and Estrellita Rivera died and so did a large part of me.

There was a departmental investigation which ended with me being completely exonerated and even awarded a commendation, and a little while after that I resigned from the force and separated from Anita and moved to my hotel on Fifty-seventh Street. I don't know how it all fits together, or if it all fits together, but what it seemed to add up to was that I hadn't enjoyed being a cop anymore. But none of this was any of Jerry Broadfield's business, and he wasn't going to hear it from me.

So I said, 'I don't really know what I can do for you.'

'You can do more than I can. You're not stuck in this lousy apartment.'

'Who brings you your food?'

'My food? Oh. I been getting out for a bite and like that. But not much and not often. And I'm careful that nobody's watching when I leave the building or come back into it.'

36

'Sooner or later somebody's going to tag you.'

'Hell, I know that.' He lit another cigarette. The gold Dunhill was just a flat sliver of metal, lost in his large hand. 'I'm just trying to buy myself a couple of days,' he said. 'That's about all. She splashed herself all over the papers yesterday. I been here since then. I figure I can last the week if I get lucky, a quiet neighborhood like this. By then maybe you can pinch her fuse.'

'Or maybe I can't do a thing.'

'Will you try, Matt?'

I didn't really want to. I was running low on money, but that didn't bother me too much. It was the beginning of the month and my rent was paid through the end of the month and I had enough cash on hand to keep me in bourbon and coffee, with a little left over for luxuries like food.

I didn't like the big cocky son of a bitch. But that didn't get in the way. As a matter of fact, I generally prefer to work for men I neither like nor respect. It pains me less to give them poor value.

So it didn't matter that I didn't like Broadfield. Or that I didn't believe that more than 20 percent of what he had told me was the truth. And I wasn't even sure which 20 percent to believe.

That last may have been what made my decision for me. Because I evidently wanted to find out what was true and what was false about Jerome Broadfield. And why he had wound up in bed with Abner Prejanian, and just where Portia Carr fit into the picture, and who was setting him up, and how and why. I don't know why I wanted to know all this, but evidently I did.

'Okay,' I said.

'You'll take a shot at it?'

I nodded.

'You'll want some money.'

I nodded again.

'How much?'

I never know how to set a fee. It didn't sound as though it would take too much time – I'd either find a way to help him or I wouldn't, and either way I'd know soon enough. But I didn't want to price myself cheap. Because I didn't like him. Because he was slick and he wore expensive clothes and he lit his cigarettes with a gold Dunhill.

'Five hundred dollars.'

He thought it seemed pretty steep. I told him he could find somebody else if he wanted. He was quick to assure me he hadn't meant anything of the sort, and he took a wallet from his inside breast pocket and counted out twenties and fifties. There was still a lot left in the wallet after he'd piled five hundred dollars on the table in front of him.

'Hope you don't mind cash,' he said.

I told him cash was fine.

'Not too many people mind,' he said, and he gave me the grin again. I just sat there for a minute or two looking at him. Then I leaned over and picked up the money.

FOUR

Its official name is the Manhattan House of Detention for Men, but I don't think I've ever heard anyone call it that. Everybody calls it the Tombs. I don't know why. But the name somehow fits the washed-out, bottomed-out, burned-out feeling of the structure and its inhabitants.

It's on White Street at Centre, conveniently located near Police Headquarters and the Criminal Courts Building. Every once in a while it gets into the papers and the television news because there's a riot there. Then the citizenry is treated to a report on the appalling conditions, and a lot of good people sign petitions, and someone appoints an investigative commission, and a lot of politicians call press conferences, and the guards ask for a pay increase, and after a few weeks it all blows over.

I don't suppose it's much worse than most urban jails. The suicide rate is high, but that's in part a result of the propensity of Puerto Rican males between the ages of eighteen and twenty-five to hang themselves in their cells for no particular reason – unless you call being Puerto Rican and in a cell adequate reason to kill yourself. Blacks and whites in that age group and those circumstances also kill themselves, but the PRs have a much higher rate, and New York has more of them than most cities.

Another thing that boosts the rate is that the guards at the Tombs wouldn't lose any sleep if every Puerto Rican in America wound up swinging from the light fixtures.

I got to the Tombs around ten-thirty after spending a few hours not getting back to sleep and not coming entirely awake either. I'd grabbed some breakfast and read the *Times* and the *News* without learning anything very exciting about Broadfield or the girl he was supposed to have killed. The *News* at least had the story, and of course they'd given it the headline and a big splash on page three. Portia Carr had not been strangled if I was to believe the newspaper; instead someone had brained her with something heavy and then stuck her in the heart with something sharp.

Broadfield had said on the phone that he thought she'd been strangled. Which meant he might have been being cute, or he might have had the story wrong, or the *News* was full of crap.

That was about all the *News* had, right or wrong. The rest was background. Even so, they were ahead of the *Times* – the late city edition didn't have a line of type on the murder.

They let me see him in his cell. He was wearing a windowpane-check suit, light blue on navy, over another custom shirt. You get to keep your own clothing if you're being held for trial. If you're serving a sentence in the Tombs you wear standard prison issue. In Broadfield's case this wouldn't happen because if he was convicted he would be sent upstate to Sing Sing or

Dannemora or Attica. You don't do murder time in the Tombs.

A guard opened his door and locked me in with him. We looked each other over without saying anything until the guard was presumably out of earshot. Then he said, 'Jesus, you came.'

'I said I would.'

'Yeah, but I didn't know whether to believe you or not. When you take a look around and realize you're locked up in a jail cell, that you're a prisoner, that something you never believed could happen to you is actually happening, shit, Matt, you don't know what to believe anymore about anything.' He took a pack of cigarettes from his pocket and offered it to me. I shook my head. He lit himself a cigarette with the gold lighter, then weighed the lighter in his hand. 'They let me hang onto this,' he said. 'That surprised me. I didn't think they let you have a lighter or matches.'

'Maybe they trust you.'

'Oh, sure.' He gestured to the bed. 'I'd say take a chair but they didn't give me one. You're welcome to the bed. Of course there's a good chance there are little creatures living in it.'

'I'm comfortable standing.'

'Yeah, so am I. It's going to be a real picnic, sleeping in that bed tonight. Why couldn't the fuckers at least give me a chair to sit on? You know, they took my tie.'

'I guess that's standard procedure.'

'No question. I had an advantage, you know. The minute I walked in the door I knew I was going to wind up in a cell. At the time I didn't know anything about Portia, that she was there, that she was dead, anything. But as soon as I saw them I knew I was going to be arrested because of the complaint she swore out. Right? So while they're asking me questions I'm taking off my jacket, getting out of my pants, kicking my shoes off. You know why?'

'Why?'

'Because they have to let you get dressed. If you're dressed to begin with they can take you that way, but if you're not they have to let you put something on, they can't haul you downtown in your underwear. So they let me get dressed and I picked out a suit with beltless slacks.' He opened the jacket to show me. 'And a pair of loafers. See?' He hiked a trouser leg to display a navy shoe. The leather looked to be lizard. 'I knew they'd want to take my belt and shoelaces. So I picked out clothes that didn't call for a belt or laces.'

'But you wore a tie.'

He gave me the old grin again. It was the first I'd seen of it this morning. 'Damn right I did. You know why?'

'Why?'

'Because I'm going to get out of here. You're gonna help me, Matt. I didn't do it and you'll find a way to prove it, and as much as they'll hate the idea they're gonna have to let me out. And when they do they'll give me back my watch and my wallet, and I'll put my watch on my wrist and my wallet in my pocket. And they'll give me my tie, and I'll get in front of a mirror and take my time getting the knot just right. I might tie it three or four times to get that knot just the way I like it. And then I'll walk out that front door and down those stone steps looking like a million dollars. And that's why I wore that fucking tie.'

The speech probably did him some good. If nothing else it reminded him that he was a class guy, a guy with style, and that was a useful self-image for him to have in a jail cell. He squared his big shoulders and got the whine of self-pity out of his voice, and I took out my notebook and gave him some questions to answer. The answers weren't all that bad, but they didn't do much to get him off the hook.

He had gone out for a sandwich not long after I'd talked to him, say around six-thirty. He'd bought a sandwich and a few bottles of beer at a delicatessen on Grove Street and brought them back to his apartment. Then he sat around listening to the radio and drinking the beer until the phone rang again a little before midnight.

'I figured it was you,' he said. 'Nobody ever calls me there. The phone's not listed. I figured it was you.'

But it was a voice he didn't recognize. A male voice, and it sounded as though it was being purposely disguised. The caller said he could get Portia Carr to change her mind and drop her charges. Broadfield was to go immediately to a bar on Ovington Avenue in the Bay Ridge section of Brooklyn. He was to sit at the bar and drink beer until somebody got in touch with him.

'To get you away from the apartment,' I said. 'Maybe they were too cute. If you can prove you were at the bar, and if the timing's right—'

'There was no bar, Matt.'

'Huh?'

43

'I shoulda known better than to go in the first place. But I figured what could I lose, right? If someone wants to arrest me and they already know about my apartment, they don't have to get cute like that, right? So I took a subway out to Bay Ridge and I found Ovington Avenue. You know Brooklyn at all?'

'Not very well.'

'Neither do I. I found Ovington, and this bar's not where it's supposed to be, so I figured I must of fucked up, and I looked in the Brooklyn Yellow Pages and it's not listed, but I keep scouting around, you know, and I finally give up and head back home. At this point I figured I was being set up for something or other, but I still can't spot the angle. Then I walk into my apartment and there's cops all over the place, and then I find out Portia's in the corner with a sheet over her, and that's why some son of a bitch wanted me chasing my tail in Bay Ridge. But there's no bartender could swear I was there because there was no bar called the High Pocket Lounge. There were a couple other bars I hit while I was there, but I couldn't tell you the names. And it wouldn't prove a thing.'

'Maybe one of the bartenders could recognize you.'

'And be positive about the time? And even so, it doesn't prove anything, Matt. I took the subway both ways, and the trains ran slow. Say I took a cab to try and set an alibi. Hell, even with the way the trains ran I could have killed Portia in my apartment around eleven-thirty before I even left for Bay Ridge. Except that she wasn't there when I left. Except that I didn't kill her.'

'Who did?'

'It's pretty obvious, isn't it? Somebody who wants to see me locked up for murder where I can't slip the shaft to the good old NYPD. Now who would want to see that happen? Who'd have a reason?'

I looked at him for a minute, then let my eyes slide off to the side. I asked him who knew about the apartment.

'Nobody.'

'That's crap. Doug Fuhrmann knew – he took me there. I knew. I also knew the phone number because you gave it to me. Did Fuhrmann know the number?'

'I think so. Yeah, I'm pretty sure he did.'

'Where did you and Doug get to be such good friends?'

'He interviewed me one time, background for a book he was writing. We got to be good drinking buddies. Why?'

'I just wondered. Who else knew about the apartment? Your wife?'

'Diana? Hell, no. She knew I had to stay over in the city from time to time, but I told her I stayed at hotels. She's the last person I'd tell about the apartment. A man tells his wife he's taking an apartment, it's only gonna mean one thing to her.' He grinned again, as abruptly as always. 'The funny thing is I took the fucking apartment primarily so I'd have a place to catch a little sleep when I wanted. A place to keep a change of clothes and like that. As far as taking broads to the apartment, I hardly ever did that. They'd generally have a place of their own.'

'But you took some women there.'

'Now and then. Meet a married woman in a bar, that

sort of thing. Most of the time they'd never know my name.'

'Who else did you take there that might know your name? Portia Carr?'

He hesitated, which was as good as an answer. 'She had a place of her own.'

'But you also took her to the place on Barrow Street.'

'Just once or twice. But she wouldn't get me out of there and then sneak in and knock herself off, would she?'

I let it go. He tried to think of anybody else who might know about the apartment and he didn't come up with anything. And as far as he knew, only Fuhrmann and I knew that he was hiding out in the apartment.

'But anybody who knew about the apartment could have guessed, Matt. All they had to do was pick up the phone and take a shot at it. And anybody could just find out about the apartment talking to some broad in a bar that I might not even remember. 'Oh, I'll bet that bastard's hiding out in that apartment of his' – and then somebody else knows about the place.'

'Did Prejanian's office know about the apartment?'

'Why the hell should they know?'

'Did you speak to them after Carr brought charges against you?'

He shook his head. 'What for? The minute her story hit the papers I ceased to exist for the son of a bitch. No point looking to him for help. All Mr Clean wants is to be the first Armenian elected governor of the state of New York. He's had his eye on Albany all along. He wouldn't be the first guy to make a trip up the Hudson on the strength of a reputation as a crime fighter.'

'I could probably think of one myself.'

'I'm not surprised. No, if I'd got Portia to change her story, Prejanian would be glad enough to see me. Now she'll never change her story and he'll never try to do me any good. Maybe I'da been better off with Hardesty.'

'Hardesty?'

'Knox Hardesty. US District Attorney. At least he's federal. He's an ambitious son of a bitch himself, but he might do me more good than Prejanian.'

'How does Hardesty come into the picture?'

'He doesn't.' He walked over to the narrow bed, sat down on it. He lit another cigarette and blew out a cloud of smoke. 'They let me bring a carton of cigarettes,' he said. 'I guess if you gotta be in jail it could be worse.'

'Why did you mention Hardesty?'

'I thought about going to him. As a matter of fact I sounded him out but he wasn't interested. He's into municipal corruption but only in a political way. Police corruption doesn't interest him.'

'So he sent you to Prejanian.'

'Are you kidding?' He seemed amazed that I would suggest anything of the sort. 'Prejanian's a Republican,' he said. 'Hardesty's a Democrat. They'd both like to be governor and they might wind up running against each other in a couple of years. You think Hardesty would send anything to Prejanian? Hardesty more or less told me to go home and soak my head. Going to Abner was my idea.'

'And you went because you just couldn't stand the corruption another minute.'

He looked at me. 'That's as good a reason as any,' he said levelly.

'If you say so.'

'I say so.' His nostrils flared. 'What difference does it make why I went to Prejanian? He's done with me now. Whoever framed me got just what he wanted. Unless you can find a way to turn it inside out.' He was on his feet now, gesturing with the cigarettes. 'You have to find out who set me up and how it was done because nothing else really gets me off the hook. I could beat this thing in court, but there would always be a cloud over me. People would just figure I got lucky in court. How many people can you think of who went up on charges for capital crimes that got a lot of heat? And when they got off, you and everybody else takes it for granted they were guilty? They say you don't get away with murder, Matt, but how many names do you know of people you'd swear got away with murder?'

I thought about it. 'I could name a dozen names,' I said. 'And that's off the top of my head.'

'Right. And if you included ones where you think they're *probably* guilty, you could name six dozen. All those guys that Lee Bailey defends and gets off, everybody is always positive the bastards are guilty. More than once I heard cops say So-and-so must be guilty or why would he need Bailey to defend him?'

'I've heard the same line.'

'Of course. My lawyer's supposed to be good, but I need more than a lawyer. Because I want more than

48

acquittal. And I can't get anything out of the cops. The ones who caught this case love it just the way it is. Nothing makes them happier than seeing me with my head on the block. So why should they look any further? All they'll look for is more ways to nail me to the wall. And if they find anything that hurts their case, you can guess what they'll do with it. They'll bury it so deep it'd be easier to reach if you started digging in China.'

We went over a few more things and I wrote down various items in my notebook. I got his home address in Forest Hills, his wife's name, the name of his lawyer, and other bits and pieces. He took a blank sheet of paper from my notebook, borrowed my pen, and wrote out an authorization for his wife to give me twenty-five hundred dollars.

'In cash, Matt. And there's more money if that's not enough. Spend what you have to. I'll back you all the way. Just fix it so I can put that tie on and get the hell out of here.'

'Where does all the money come from?'

He looked at me. 'Does it matter?'

'I don't know.'

'What the fuck am I supposed to say? That I saved it out of my salary? You know better than that. I already told you I was never a Boy Scout.'

'Uh-huh.'

'Does it matter where the money came from?'

I thought about it. 'No,' I said. 'No, I don't guess it does.'

★

On our way back through the corridors the guard said, 'You were a cop yourself, right?'

'For a while.'

'And now you're working for him.'

'That's right.'

'Well,' he said judiciously, 'we don't always get to choose who we're gonna work for. And a man's got to make hisself a living.'

'That's the truth.'

He whistled softly. He was in his late fifties, jowly and round-shouldered, with liver spots on the backs of his hands. His voice had been roughened by years of whiskey and tobacco.

'Figure to get him off?'

'I'm no lawyer. If I can turn up some evidence, maybe his lawyer can get him off. Why?'

'Just thinking. If he don't get off, he's apt to wish they still had capital punishment.'

'Why's that?'

'He's a cop, ain't he?'

'So?'

'Well, you just think on it. The present time, we got him in a cell by his lonesome. Awaiting trial and all of that, wearin' his own clothes, keepin' to hisself. But let's just say he's convicted and he's sent up to, say, Attica. And there he is in a prison full to overflowing with criminals who got no use at all for the police, and better'n half of 'em coons who was born hating the police. Now there is all kinds of ways to do time, but do you know any harder time than that poor bastard is going to serve?'

'I hadn't thought of that.'

The guard clucked his tongue against the roof of his mouth. 'Why, he'll never have a minute when he won't have to be worryin' about some black bastard comin' at him with a homemade knife. They steal spoons from the mess hall and grind 'em down in the machine shop, you know. I worked Attica some years ago, I know how they do things there. You recall the big riot? When they seized the hostages and all? I was long out of there by that time, but I knew two of the guards who was taken as hostages and killed. That's a hell of a place, that Attica. Your buddy Broadfield gets hisself sent there, I'd say he's lucky if he's alive after two years.'

We walked the rest of the way in silence. As he was about to leave me he said, 'Hardest kind of time in the world is the time a cop serves in a prison. But I got to say the bastard deserves it if anybody does.'

'Maybe he didn't kill the girl.'

'Oh, shoot,' he said. 'Who cares a damn if he killed her? He went and turned on his own kind, didn't he? He's a traitor to his badge, ain't he? I don't care a damn about some filthy prostitute and who killed her or didn't kill her. That bastard in there deserves whatever he gets.'

FIVE

I went there first because of the locations. The Tombs is on White at Centre, and Abner Prejanian and his eager beavers had a suite of offices four blocks away on Worth between Church and Broadway. The building was a narrow yellow brickfront which Prejanian shared with a couple of accountants, a photocopying service, some import–export people, and, on the ground floor, a shop that repaired shoes and reblocked hats. I climbed steep stairs that squeaked, and too many of them; if he'd been a flight higher I might have given up and turned around. But I got to his floor and a door was open and I walked in.

On Tuesday, after my first meeting with Jerry Broadfield, I had spent almost two dollars' worth of dimes trying to reach Portia Carr. Not all at once, of course, but a dime at a time. She had had an answering machine, and when you reach an answering machine from a public phone you usually lose your dime. If you hang up fast enough, and if you're lucky and your reflexes are good, you get your dime back. As the day wears on, this happens less and less frequently.

When I wasn't wasting dimes that day I tried a few other approaches, and one of them involved a girl named Elaine Mardell. She was in the same line of work as Portia Carr and lived in the same neighborhood. I went over to see Elaine, and she managed to tell me a few things about Portia. Nothing firsthand – she hadn't known her personally – but some gossip she had heard at one time or other. That Portia had specialized in SM fantasy fulfillment, that she was supposedly turning down dates lately, and that she had a 'special friend' who was prominent or notorious or influential or something.

The girl in Prejanian's office looked enough like Elaine to be her sister. She frowned at me and I realized that I was staring at her. A second glance showed me that she didn't really resemble Elaine that closely. The similarity was mostly in the eyes. She had the same dark deep-set Jewish eyes and they dominated her entire face in much the same way.

She asked if she could help me. I said I wanted to see Mr Prejanian and she asked if I had an appointment. I admitted I didn't, and she said he was out to lunch, as were most of his staff. I decided not to assume she was a secretary just because she was a woman, and started to tell her what I wanted.

'I'm just a secretary,' she said. 'Do you want to wait until Mr Prejanian gets back? Or there's Mr Lorbeer. I believe he's in his office.'

'Who's Mr Lorbeer?'

'Staff assistant to Mr Prejanian.'

That still didn't tell me a great deal, but I asked to see him. She invited me to have a seat, pointing to a wooden folding chair that looked about as inviting as the bed in Broadfield's cell. I stayed on my feet.

A few minutes later I was sitting across an old oak veneer desk from Claude Lorbeer. When I was a kid, every schoolroom I was ever in had a desk just like that for the teacher. I'd had only female teachers except for gym and shop, but if I'd had a male classroom teacher he might have looked something like Lorbeer, who certainly looked at home behind that desk. He had short, dark brown hair and a narrow mouth with deeply etched lines like paired parentheses on either side of it. His hands were plump with short, stubby fingers. They were pale and looked soft. He wore a white shirt and a solid maroon tie and he had his shirt-sleeves rolled up. Something about him made me feel as though I must have done something wrong, and that my not knowing what it might be was no excuse at all.

'Mr Scudder,' he said. 'I suppose you're the officer I spoke to over the telephone this morning. I can only repeat what I said earlier. Mr Prejanian has no information to make available to the police. Any criminous action which Mr Broadfield may have performed is beyond the scope of this investigation and surely not in any way known to this office. We have not yet spoken to members of the press but will of course take the same tack with them. We will decline to comment and will stress that Mr Broadfield had volunteered to make certain information available to us but that we had taken no action in respect to information furnished by him nor do we anticipate so doing while Mr Broadfield's legal status is undefined as it is at present.'

He said all of this as though he was reading it from a prepared text. Most people have trouble speaking in sentences. Lorbeer spoke in paragraphs, structurally complicated paragraphs, and he delivered his little speech with his pale eyes fixed on the tip of my left shoulder.

I said, 'I think you've jumped to a conclusion. I'm not a cop.'

'You're from the press? I thought—'

'I used to be a cop. I left the force a couple of years ago.'

His face took on an interesting cast at this news. There was some calculation in it. I got a rush of *déjà vu* looking at him, and it took me a minute to put it in place. He reminded me of Broadfield at our first meeting, head cocked to the side and face screwed up in concentration. Like Broadfield, Lorbeer wanted to know what my angle was. He might be a reformer, he might be working for Mr Clean himself, but in his own way he was as much on the make as a cop looking for a handout.

'I've just been to see Broadfield,' I said. 'I'm working for him. He says he didn't kill the Carr woman.'

'Naturally he'd say that, wouldn't he? I understand her body was found in his apartment.'

I nodded. 'He figures he was deliberately framed for her murder. He wants me to try and find out who framed him.'

'I see.' He was somewhat less interested in me now since I was just trying to solve a murder. He'd been hoping I was going to help him louse up an entire police department. 'Well, I'm not certain how our office would be involved.'

'Maybe you're not. I just want a fuller picture. I don't know Broadfield well, I just met him the first time Tuesday. He's a tricky customer. I can't always tell when he's lying to me.'

A trace of a smile appeared on Claude Lorbeer's lips.

It looked out of place there. 'I like the way you put it,' he said. 'He *is* a subtle liar, isn't he?'

'That's what's hard to tell. How subtle is he, and how much does he lie? He says he just came over and volunteered his services to you people. That you didn't have to force him into it.'

'That's quite true.'

'It's hard to believe.'

Lorbeer made a tent of his fingertips. 'No harder for you than for us,' he said. 'Broadfield just walked in off the street. He didn't even call first to tell us he was coming. We'd never heard of him before he barged in offering us the earth and asking nothing in return.'

'That doesn't make sense.'

'I *know* it.' He leaned forward, his expression one of great concentration. I suppose he was about twenty-eight. His manner put extra years on him, but when he grew intense those years dropped away and you realized how young he was underneath it all. 'That's what makes it so difficult to place credence in anything the man says, Mr Scudder. One can see no possible motivation for him. Oh, he asked for immunity from prosecution for anything he might disclose that implicated himself, but we grant that automatically. But he didn't want anything beyond that.'

'Then why did he come here?'

'I have no idea. I'll tell you something. I distrusted him immediately. Not because he's crooked. We deal with crooks all the time. We have to deal with crooks, but at least they are rational crooks, and his behavior was irrational. I told Mr Prejanian that I didn't trust

Broadfield. I said I felt he was a kook, an oddball. I didn't want to get involved with him at all.'

'And you said as much to Prejanian.'

'Yes, I did. I would have been happy to believe that Broadfield had had some sort of religious experience and turned into a completely new person. Perhaps that sort of thing happens. Not very often, I don't suppose.'

'Probably not.'

'But he didn't even pretend that was the case. He was the same man he'd been before, cynical and breezy and very much the operator.' He sighed. 'Now Mr Prejanian agrees with me. He's sorry we ever got involved with Broadfield. The man's evidently committed a murder, and, oh, even before that there was the unfortunate publicity which resulted from the charges that woman brought against him. It could all put us in something of a delicate position. We didn't *do* anything, you know, but the publicity can hardly work to our advantage.'

I nodded. 'About Broadfield,' I said. 'Did you see him often?'

'Not very often. He worked directly with Mr Prejanian.'

'Did he ever bring anyone to this office? A woman?'

'No, he was always alone.'

'Did Prejanian or anyone from this office ever meet him elsewhere?'

'No, he always came here.'

'Do you know where his apartment was?'

'Barrow Street, wasn't it?' I perked up at that, but then he said, 'I didn't even know he had an apartment in New York, but there was something about it in the newspaper, wasn't there? I think it was someplace in Greenwich Village.'

'Did Portia Carr's name ever come up?'

'That's the woman he murdered, isn't it?'

'That's the woman who was murdered.'

He managed a smile. 'I stand corrected. I suppose one cannot jump to conclusions, however obvious they seem. No, I'm sure I never heard her name before that item appeared in Monday's newspaper.'

I showed him Portia's photo, torn from the morning's *News*. I added some verbal description. But he had never seen her before.

'Let me see if I have it all straight,' he said. 'He was extorting money from this woman. A hundred dollars a week, I believe it was? And she exposed him Monday, and last night she was murdered in his apartment.'

'She said he was extorting money from her. I met her and she told me the same story. I think she was lying.'

'Why would she lie?'

'To discredit Broadfield.'

He seemed genuinely puzzled. 'But why would she want to do that? She was a prostitute, wasn't she? Why should a prostitute try to impede our crusade against police corruption? And why would someone else murder a prostitute in Broadfield's apartment? It's all very confusing.'

'Well, I won't argue with you on that.'

'Terribly confusing,' he said. 'I can't even understand why Broadfield came to us in the first place.'

I could. At least I had a good idea now. But I decided to keep it to myself.

SIX

I stopped at my hotel long enough to take a quick shower and run an electric razor over my face. There were three messages in my pigeonhole, three callers who wanted to be called back. Anita had called again, and a police lieutenant named Eddie Koehler. And Miss Mardell.

I decided that Anita and Eddie could wait. I called Elaine from the pay phone in the lobby. It wasn't a call I wanted to route through the hotel switchboard. Maybe they don't listen in, but then again maybe they do.

When she answered I said, 'Hello. Do you know who this is?'

'I think so.'

'I'm returning your call.'

'Uh-huh. Thought so. You got phone troubles?'

'I'm in a booth, but how about you?'

'This phone's supposed to be clean. I pay this little Hawaiian cat to come over once a week and check for bugs. So far he hasn't found any, but maybe he doesn't know how to look. How would I know? He's really a very little cat. I think he must be completely transistorized.'

'You're a funny lady.'

'Well, where are we without a sense of humor, huh? But we might as well be reasonably cool on the phone. You can probably guess what I called about.'

'Uh-huh.'

'The questions you were asking the other day, and I'm a girl who reads the paper every morning, and what I was wondering was, can any of this lead back to me? Is that something I should start worrying about?'

'Not a chance.'

'Is that straight?'

'Absolutely. Unless some of the calls you made to find things out can work back toward you. You talked to some people.'

'I already thought of that and sealed it off. If you say I got nothing to worry about, then I don't, and that's the way Mrs Mardell's little girl likes it.'

'I thought you changed your name.'

'Huh? Oh, no, not me. I was born Elaine Mardell, baby. Not saying my father didn't change it a while back, but it was already nice and goyish by the time I came on the scene.'

'I might come over later, Elaine.'

'Business or pleasure? Let me reword that. Your business or mine?'

I found myself smiling into the telephone. 'Maybe a little of both,' I said. 'I have to go out to Queens, but I'll give you a call afterward if I'm coming.'

'Call me either way, baby. If you can't come, call. That's why they put—'

'Dimes in condoms. I know.'

'Awww, you know all my best jokes,' she said. 'You're no fun at all.'

My subway car had been decorated by a lunatic with a can of spray paint. He'd had just one message for the world and he had taken pains to inscribe it wherever the opportunity had presented itself, restating his argument over and over again, working in elaborate curlicues and other embellishments.

WE ARE PEOPLE TWO, he informed us. I couldn't decide whether the last word was a simple spelling error or represented some significant drug-inspired insight.

WE ARE PEOPLE TWO.

I had plenty of time to ponder the meaning of the phrase, all the way out to Queens Boulevard and Continental. I got off the train and walked for several blocks, passing streets named after prep schools. Exeter, Groton, Harrow. I eventually got to Nansen Street, where Broadfield and his family lived. I don't know how they named Nansen Street.

The Broadfield house was a good one, set back on a nicely landscaped lot. An old maple on the strip of lawn between the sidewalk and the street left no doubt about what time of year it was. It was all on fire with red and gold.

The house itself was two storeys tall and thirty or forty years old. It had aged well. The whole block was composed of similar houses, but they differed sufficiently so that one didn't have the sense of being in a development.

Nor did I have the sense of being within the five boroughs of New York. It is hard to remember, living in Manhattan, just how high a percentage of New Yorkers inhabit one-family houses on tree-lined streets. Even politicians sometimes have trouble keeping this in mind.

I walked up a flagstone path to the front door and

rang the bell. I could hear chimes sounding inside the house. Then footsteps approached the door, and it was drawn open by a slender woman with short dark hair. She wore a lime-green sweater and dark green pants. Green was a good color for her, matching her eyes, pointing up the shy wood-nymph quality she projected. She was attractive and would have been prettier still if she hadn't been crying recently. Her eyes were rimmed with red and her face was drawn.

I told her my name and she invited me inside. She said I would have to excuse her, that everything was a mess because it had been a bad day for her.

I followed her into the living room and took the chair she indicated. Despite what she'd said, nothing seemed to be a mess. The room was immaculate and very tastefully furnished. The decor was conservative and traditional without having a museum feel to it. There were photographs here and there in silver frames. A book of music stood open on the upright piano. She picked it up, closed it, put it away in the piano bench.

'The children are upstairs,' she said. 'Sara and Jennifer went to school this morning. They left before I heard the news. When they came home from lunch I kept them home. Eric won't start kindergarten until next year, so he's used to being at home. I don't know what they're thinking and I don't know what to say to them. And the telephone keeps ringing. I'd love to take it off the hook, but what if it's something important? I would have missed your call if I'd taken it off the hook. I just wish I knew what to do.' She winced and wrung her hands. 'I'm sorry,' she said, her voice steadier now.

'I'm in a state of shock. It's made me numb and jittery at the same time. For two days I didn't know where my husband was. Now I know that he's in a prison cell. And charged with murder.' She made herself take a breath. 'Would you like some coffee? I just made a fresh pot. Or I could give you something stronger.'

I said that coffee with whiskey in it would be good. She went to the kitchen and came back with two large mugs of coffee. 'I don't know what kind of whiskey or how much to put in,' she said. 'There's the liquor cabinet. Why don't you pick out what you like?'

The cabinet was well stocked with expensive brands. This did not surprise me. I never knew a cop who didn't get a lot of liquor at Christmas. The people who are a little diffident about giving you cash find it easier to give you a bottle or a case of decent booze. I put a healthy slug of Wild Turkey in my cup. I suppose it was a waste. One bourbon tastes pretty much like another when you pour it in coffee.

'Is it good that way?' She was standing beside me, her own mug held in both hands. 'Maybe I'll try some. I don't normally drink very much. I've never liked the taste of it. Do you think a drink would relax me?'

'It probably wouldn't hurt.'

She held out her mug. 'Please?'

I filled her mug and she stirred it with her spoon and took a tentative sip. 'Oh, that's good,' she said, in what was almost a child's voice. 'It's warming, isn't it? Is it very potent?'

'It's about the same strength as a cocktail. And the coffee tends to counteract some of the effects of the alcohol.'

'You mean you don't get drunk?'

'You still get drunk eventually. But you don't get tired out en route. Do you normally get drunk on one drink?'

'I can usually *feel* one drink. I'm afraid I'm not much of a drinker. But I don't suppose this will hurt me.'

She looked at me, and for a short moment we challenged one another with our eyes. I didn't know then and do not know now precisely what happened, but our eyes met and exchanged wordless messages, and something must have been settled on the spot, although we were not consciously aware of the settlement or even of the messages that preceded it.

I broke the stare. I took the note her husband had written from my wallet and handed it to her. She scanned it once quickly, then read it through more carefully. 'Twenty-five hundred dollars,' she said. 'I suppose you'll want that right now, Mr Scudder.'

'I'll probably be having some expenses.'

'Certainly.' She folded the note in two, then folded it again. 'I don't recall Jerry mentioning your name. Have you known each other for a long time?'

'Not long at all.'

'You're on the force. Did you work together?'

'I used to be on the force, Mrs Broadfield. Now I'm a sort of private detective.'

'Just sort of?'

'The unlicensed sort. After all those years in the department I have an aversion to filling out forms.'

'An aversion.'

'Pardon me?'

'Did I say that aloud?' She smiled suddenly and her

whole face brightened. 'I don't think I've ever heard a policeman use that word. Oh, they use large words, but of a certain sort, you know. "Alleged perpetrator" is my favorite phrase of all. And "miscreant" is a wonderful word. Nobody but a policeman or a reporter ever called anybody a miscreant, and reporters just write it, they never say it out loud.' Our eyes locked again and her smile faded out. 'I'm sorry, Mr Scudder. I'm babbling again, aren't I?'

'I like the way you babble.'

For a second I thought she was going to blush, but she didn't. She took a breath and assured me I would have my money in a moment. I said there was no rush but she said it would be just as easy to get it over and done with. I sat down and worked on my coffee and she left the room and climbed a flight of stairs.

She returned a few minutes later with a sheaf of bills which she handed to me. I fanned them. They were all fifties and hundreds. I put them in my jacket pocket.

'Aren't you going to count them?' I shook my head. 'You're very trusting, Mr Scudder. I'm sure you told me your first name but I don't seem to remember it.'

'Matthew.'

'Mine is Diana.' She picked up her coffee mug and drained it quickly, as if downing strong medicine. 'Will it be helpful if I say my husband was with me last night?'

'He was arrested in New York, Mrs Broadfield.'

'I just told you my name. Aren't you going to use it?' Then she remembered what we were talking about and her tone changed. 'What time was he arrested?'

'Around two-thirty.'

'Where?'

'An apartment in the Village. He'd been staying there ever since Miss Carr brought those charges against him. He was decoyed out of there last night, and while he was out somebody brought the Carr woman to his apartment and killed her there and tipped the police. Or brought her there after she was dead.'

'Or Jerry killed her.'

'It doesn't make sense that way.'

She thought about this, then took up another tack. 'Whose apartment was it?'

'I'm not sure.'

'Really? It must have been his apartment. Oh, I've always been sure he has one. There are clothes of his I haven't seen in ages, so I gather he keeps part of his wardrobe somewhere in the city.' She sighed. 'I wonder why he tries to hide things from me. I know so much and he must know that I know, don't you suppose? Does he think I don't know that he has other women? Does he think I care?'

'Don't you?'

She looked long and hard at me. I didn't think she was going to answer the question, but then she did. 'Of course I care,' she said. 'Of course I care.' She looked down at her coffee mug and seemed dismayed to see that it was empty. 'I'm going to have some more coffee,' she said. 'Would you like some, Matthew?'

'Thank you.'

She carried the mugs to the kitchen. On the way back she stopped at the liquor cabinet to doctor them both. She had a generous hand with the Wild Turkey bottle, making my drink at least twice as strong as the one I'd made for myself.

She sat on the couch again, but this time she placed herself closer to my chair. She sipped her coffee and looked at me over the top of her mug. 'What time was that girl killed?'

'According to the last news I heard, they're estimating the time of death at midnight.'

'And he was arrested around two-thirty?'

'Around that time, yes.'

'Well, that makes it simple, doesn't it? I'll say that he came home just after the children went to sleep. He wanted to see me and change his clothing. And he was with me, watching television from eleven o'clock until the Carson show went off, and then he went back to New York and got there just in time to get arrested. What's the matter?'

'It won't do any good, Diana.'

'Why not?'

'Nobody'll buy it. The only kind of alibi that'd do your husband any good would be an ironclad one, and the uncorroborated word of his wife — no, it wouldn't do any good.'

'I suppose I must have known that.'

'Sure.'

'Did he kill her, Matthew?'

'He says he didn't.'

'Do you believe him?'

I nodded. 'I believe someone else killed her. And deliberately framed him for it.'

'Why?'

'To stop the investigation into the police depart-ment. Or for private reasons – if someone had cause to kill Portia Carr, your husband certainly made a perfect fall guy.'

'That's not what I meant. What makes *you* believe he's innocent?'

I thought about it. I had some fairly good reasons – among them the fact that he was too bright to commit murder in quite so stupid a fashion. He might kill the woman in his own apartment, but he wouldn't leave her there and spend a couple of hours drifting around without even establishing an alibi. But none of my reasons really mattered all that much and they weren't worth repeating to her.

'I just don't believe he did it. I was a cop for a long time. You develop instincts, intuition. Things have a certain feel to them, and if you're any good you know how to pick up on them.'

'I'll bet you were good.'

'I wasn't bad. I had the moves, I had the instincts. And I was so involved in what I was doing that I wound up using a lot of myself in my work. That makes a difference. It becomes much easier to be good at something that you're really caught up in.'

'And then you left the force?'

'Yes. A few years ago.'

'Voluntarily?' She colored and put a hand to her lips. 'I'm very sorry,' she said. 'That's a stupid question and it's none of my business.'

'It's not stupid. Yes, I left voluntarily.'

'Why? Not that that's any of my business, either.'

'Private reasons.'

'Of course. I'm terribly sorry, I think I *am* feeling this whiskey. Forgive me?'

'Nothing to forgive. The reasons are private, that's all. Maybe I'll like telling you about it someday.'

'Maybe you will, Matt.'

And our eyes got connected again and stayed locked until she abruptly drew a breath and finished the liquid in her coffee mug.

She said, 'Did you take money? I mean, when you were on the force.'

'Some. I didn't get rich at it, and I didn't go out looking for it, but I took what came my way. We never lived on my salary.'

'You're married?'

'Oh, because I said *we*. I'm divorced.'

'Sometimes I think about divorce. I can't think about it now, of course. Now it is incumbent upon the faithful, long-suffering wife to remain at her husband's side in his hour of need. Why are you smiling?'

'I'll trade you three aversions for one incumbent.'

'It's a trade.' She lowered her eyes. 'Jerry takes a lot of money,' she said.

'So I've gathered.'

'That money I gave you. Twenty-five hundred dollars. Imagine having so much money around the house. All I did, I just went upstairs and counted it out. There's a great deal more left in the strongbox. I don't know how much he has there. I've never counted it.'

I didn't say anything. She was sitting with her legs crossed at the knee and her hands folded neatly in her lap. Dark green pants on her long legs, bright green sweater, cool mint-green eyes. Sensitive hands with long slender fingers and closely trimmed unpolished nails.

'I never even knew about the strongbox until just before he began consulting with that Special Prosecutor. I can never remember that man's name.'

'Abner Prejanian.'

'Yes. Of course I knew Jerry took money. He never said so in so many words, but it was obvious, and he did hint at it. As if he wanted me to know but didn't want to tell me outright. It was obvious to me that we weren't living on what he earned legitimately. And he spends so much money on his clothes, and I suppose he spends money on other women.' Her voice came close to breaking, but she sailed right on as if nothing had happened. 'One day he took me aside and showed me the box. There's a combination lock, and he taught me the combination. He said I could help myself to money anytime I needed it, that there would always be more where that came from.

'I never opened the box until just now. Not to count it or anything. I didn't want to look at it, I didn't want to think about it, I didn't want to know how much money was in there. Do you want to know something interesting? One night last week I was thinking of leaving him and I couldn't imagine how I would be able to afford to do it. Financially, I mean. And I never even gave a thought to the money in the strongbox. It never occurred to me.

'I don't know if I'm a very moral person or not. I don't think I am, really. But there is so very much money there, don't you see, and I don't like to think what a person would have to have done in order to get all that money. Am I making any sense at all to you, Matt?'

'Yes.'

'Maybe he did kill that woman. If he decided he ought to kill a person, I don't think he'd have any moral compunctions about doing it.'

'Did he ever kill anyone in the line of duty?'

'No. He shot several criminals but none of them died.'

'Was he in the service?'

'He was based in Germany for a couple of years. He was never in combat.'

'Is he violent? Has he ever struck you?'

'No, never. Sometimes I've been afraid of him, but I couldn't explain why. He's never given me real reason for fear. I would leave any man who hit me.' She smiled bitterly. 'At least I think I would. But I once thought I'd leave any man who had other women. Why do we never know ourselves as well as we think we do, Matt?'

'That's a good question.'

'I have so many good questions. I don't really know that man at all. Isn't that remarkable? I've been married to him for all these years and I don't know him. I have never known him. Did he tell you why he decided to cooperate with the Special Prosecutor?'

'I was hoping he might have told you.'

She shook her head. 'And I have no idea whatsoever. But then I never know why he does things. Why did he marry me? Now there's a good question. There's what I'd call a damn good question, Matthew. What did Jerome Broadfield see in mousy little Diana Cummings?'

'Oh, come on. You must know you're attractive.'

'I know I'm not ugly.'

'You're a lot more than not ugly.' *And your hands perch upon your thigh like a pair of doves. And a man could get altogether lost in your eyes.*

'I'm not very dramatic, Matthew.'

'I don't follow you.'

'How to explain? Let me see. Do you know how some actors can just walk onto a stage and every eye is drawn to them? It doesn't matter if someone else is in the middle of a speech. They just have so much dramatic quality that you have to look at them. I'm not like that, not at all. And of course Jerry is.'

'He's striking, certainly. His height probably has something to do with it.'

'It's more than that. He's tall and good-looking but it's more than that. There's a quality he has. People look at him on the street. They always have as long as I've known him. And don't think he doesn't work at it. Sometimes I've seen him at work on it, Matthew. I'll recognize a deliberately casual gesture that I've caught him using before, and I will know just how calculated it is, and at moments like that I can honestly despise the man.'

A car passed by outside. We sat, our eyes not quite meeting, and we listened to distant street sounds and private thoughts.

'You said you were divorced.'

'Yes.'

'Recently?'

'A few years.'

'Children?'

'Two boys. My wife has custody.'

'I have two girls and a boy. I must have told you that.'

'Sara and Jennifer and Eric.'

'You have a remarkable memory.' She looked at her hands. 'Is it better? Being divorced?'

'I don't know. Sometimes it's better and sometimes it's worse. I don't actually think of it in those terms because there wasn't really any choice involved. It had to be that way.'

'Your wife wanted the divorce.'

'No, I was the one who wanted it. The one who had to live alone. But my wanting wasn't a matter of choice, if that makes any sense to you. I *had* to be by myself.'

'Are you still living alone?'

'Yes.'

'Do you enjoy it?'

'Does anyone?'

She was silent for a long moment. She sat with her hands gripping her knee, her head tilted back, her eyes closed, and her thoughts turned inward. Without opening her eyes she said, 'What's going to happen to Jerry?'

'It's impossible to say. Unless something turns up he'll go to trial. He might get off or he might not. A high-powered lawyer could drag things out for a long time.'

'But it's possible he'll be convicted?'

I hesitated, then nodded.

'And go to prison?'

'It's possible.'

'God.'

She picked up her mug and stared down into it, then raised her eyes to meet mine. 'Should I get us more coffee, Matthew?'

'No more for me.'

'Should I have some more? Should I have another drink?'

'If it's what you need.'

She thought about it. 'It's not what I need,' she decided. 'Do you know what I need?'

I didn't say anything.

'I need you to come over here and sit next to me. I need to be held.'

I sat on the couch beside her and she came into my arms eagerly like a small animal seeking warmth. Her face was very soft against mine, her breath warm and sweet. When my mouth found hers she stiffened for a moment. Then, as if realizing that her decision had long since been reached, she relaxed in my arms and returned the kiss.

At one point she said, 'Let's just make everything go away. Everything.' And then she did not have to say anything after that, and neither did I.

A little later we were sitting as before, she on the couch, I on my chair. She was sipping unspiked coffee, and I had a glass of straight bourbon that I'd finished a little more than half of. We were talking quietly and we stopped our conversation when footsteps sounded on the stairs. A girl about ten years old entered the room. She looked like her mother.

She said, 'Mommy, me and Jennifer want to—'

'Jennifer and I.'

The child sighed theatrically. 'Mommy, *Jennifer* and I want to watch *Fantastic Voyage* and Eric is being a pig and wants to watch *The Flintstones* and me and Jennifer I mean Jennifer and I hate *The Flintstones*.'

'Don't call Eric a pig.'

'I didn't *call* Eric a pig. I just said he was *being* a pig.'

'I suppose there's a difference. You and Jennifer can watch your program in my room. Is that what you wanted?'

'Why doesn't Eric watch in your room? After all, Mommy, he's watching *our* set in *our* room.'

'I don't want Eric alone in my room.'

'Well, me and Jennifer don't want him alone in *our* room, Mommy, and—'

'Sara—'

'Okay. *We'll* watch in *your* room.'

'Sara, this is Mr Scudder.'

'Hello, Mr Scudder. Can I go now, Mommy?'

'Go ahead.'

When the child had disappeared up the staircase, her mother let out a long, low-pitched whistle. 'I don't know what on earth is the matter with me,' she said. 'I've never done anything like that before. I don't mean I've been a saint. I was … last year there was someone I was involved with. But in my own house, God, and with my children at home. Sara could have walked right in on us. I'd never have heard her.' She smiled suddenly. 'I wouldn't have heard World War Three. You're a sweet man, Matthew. I don't know how this happened, but I am not going to make excuses for it. I'm *glad* it happened.'

'So am I.'

'Do you know that you still haven't spoken my name? All you've called me is Mrs Broadfield.'

I'd said her name once aloud and many times silently. But I said it again now. 'Diana.'

'That's much better.'

'Diana, goddess of the moon.'

'And of the hunt.'

'Of the hunt, too? I just knew about the moon.'

'I wonder if it will be out tonight. The moon. It's getting dark already, isn't it? I can't believe it. Where did the summer go? It was just spring the other day and now it's October. In a couple of weeks my three wild Indians will put on costumes and extort candy from the neighbors.' Her face clouded. 'It's a family tradition, after all. Extortion.'

'Diana—'

'And Thanksgiving is just a month away. Doesn't it seem as though we had Thanksgiving three months ago? Or four at the very most?'

'I know what you mean. The days take as long to pass as ever, but the years fly by.'

She nodded. 'I always thought my grandmother was crazy. She would tell me time passed much more quickly when you were older. Either she was crazy or she considered me a very gullible child because how could time possibly alter its pace according to one's age? But there *is* a difference. A year is three percent of my life and ten percent of Sara's, so of course it flies for me and crawls for her. And she's in a hurry for time to rush

76

by, and I wish it would slow itself down a bit. Oh, Matthew, it's not all that much fun getting old.'

'Silly.'

'Me? Why?'

'Talking about being old when you're just a kid yourself.'

'You can't be a kid anymore when you're somebody's mother.'

'The hell you can't.'

'And I'm getting older, Matthew. Look how much older I am today than yesterday.'

'Older? But younger, too, aren't you? In one way?'

'Oh, yes,' she said. 'Yes, you're right. And I hadn't even thought of that.'

When my glass was empty I got to my feet and told her I'd better be going. She said it would be nice if I could stay and I said it was probably a good thing that I couldn't. She thought about that and agreed it was probably true but said it would have been nice all the same.

'You'll be cold,' she said. 'It cools off quickly once the sun is down. I'll drive you to Manhattan. Shall I do that? Sara's old enough to baby-sit for that length of time. I'll run you in, it's faster than the train.'

'Let me take the train, Diana.'

'Then I'll drive you to it.'

'I'd just as soon walk off some of the booze.'

She studied me, then nodded. 'All right.'

'I'll call you as soon as I know anything.'

'Or even if you don't?'

'Or even if I don't.'

I reached out for her, but she backed away. 'I want you to know I'm not going to cling, Matthew.'

'I know that.'

'You don't have to feel you owe me anything.'

'Come here.'

'Oh, my sweet man.'

And at the door she said, 'And you'll go on working for Jerry. Is this going to complicate things?'

'Everything generally does,' I said.

It was cold outside. When I got to the corner and turned north, there was a wind with a lot of bite to it coming right up behind me. I was wearing my suit and it wasn't enough.

Halfway to the subway stop I realized I could have borrowed an overcoat of his. A man with Jerry Broadfield's enthusiasm for clothing was sure to have three or four of them, and Diana would have been happy enough to lend me one. I hadn't thought of it and she hadn't volunteered, and now I decided that it was just as well. So far today I'd sat in his chair and drunk his whiskey and taken his money and made love to his wife. I didn't have to walk around town in his clothes.

The subway platform was elevated and looked like a stop on the Long Island Rail Road. Evidently a train had just gone through, although I hadn't heard it. I was the only person waiting on the westbound platform. Gradually other people joined me and stood around smoking.

It's theoretically illegal to smoke in subway stations whether they're above or below ground. Almost everyone honors this rule below the surface of the earth, and virtually all smokers feel free to smoke on elevated platforms. I've no idea why this is so. Subway stations, above or below ground, are equally fireproof, and the air in both is so foul that smoke won't make it noticeably worse. But the law is obeyed in one type of station and routinely violated (and unenforced) in the other, and no one has ever explained why.

Curious.

The train came eventually. People threw away their cigarettes and boarded it. The car I rode in was festooned with graffiti, but the legends were limited to the now-conventional nicknames and numbers. Nothing as imaginative as WE ARE PEOPLE TWO.

I hadn't planned on fucking his wife.

There was a point where I hadn't even considered it, and another point where I knew for certain that it was going to happen, and the two points had been placed remarkably close together in time.

Hard to say exactly why it happened.

I don't all that frequently meet women I want. It is a less and less frequent occurrence, either because of some facet of the aging process or as a result of my personal metamorphoses. I had met one such woman a day ago, and for a variety of reasons, some known and some unknown, I had done nothing about it. And now she and I would never have a chance to happen to each other.

Perhaps some idiot cells in my brain had managed to convince themselves that, if I did not take Diana Broadfield on her living-room couch, some maniac would come along and slaughter her.

The car was warm but I shivered as if I were still standing on the elevated platform exposed to the sharp edge of the wind. It was the best time of the year but it was also the saddest. Because winter was coming.

SEVEN

There were more messages waiting for me at my hotel. Anita had called again and Eddie Koehler had called twice. I walked over to the elevator, then turned and used the pay phone to call Elaine.

'I said I'd call either way,' I told her. 'I don't think I'm going to drop over tonight. Maybe tomorrow.'

'Sure, Matt. Was it anything important?'

'You remember what we were talking about before. If you could find out some more on that subject I'd make it worth your while.'

'I don't know,' she said. 'I don't want to stick my neck out. I like to keep what they call a low profile. I do my work and I save my pennies for my old age.'

'Real estate, isn't it?'

'Uh-huh. Apartment houses in Queens.'

'Hard to see you as a landlady.'

'The tenants never set eyes on me. This management firm takes care of everything. The guy who handles it for me, I know him professionally.'

'Uh-huh. Getting rich?'

'Doing okay. I'm not going to be one of those old Broadway ladies with a dollar a day to feed themselves on. No way.'

'Well, you could ask a few questions and make a few dollars. If you're interested.'

'I suppose I could try. You'll keep my name out of

everything, right? You just want me to come up with something that'll give you an opening.'

'That's right.'

'Well, I could see what happens.'

'Do that, Elaine. I'll drop by tomorrow.'

'Call first.'

I went upstairs, kicked off my shoes, stretched out on the bed. I closed my eyes for a minute or two. I was just on the verge of sleep when I forced myself to sit up. The bourbon bottle on the bedside table was empty. I dropped it into the wastebasket and checked the closet shelf. There was an unopened pint of Jim Beam just waiting for me. I cracked it and took a short pull from it. It wasn't Wild Turkey but it did get the job done.

Eddie Koehler wanted me to call him but I couldn't see any reason why that conversation couldn't wait a day or two. I could guess what he was going to tell me and it wasn't anything I wanted to hear.

It must have been around a quarter after eight when I picked up the phone and called Anita.

We didn't have too much to say to each other. She told me the bills had been heavy lately, she'd had some root-canal work done and the boys seemed to be outgrowing everything at once, and if I could spare a couple of bucks it would be welcome. I said I'd just landed some work and would get a money order off to her in the morning.

'That would be a big help, Matt. But the reason I kept leaving messages for you, the boys wanted to talk to you.'

'Sure.'

I talked to Mickey first. He didn't really say much. School was fine, everything was okay – the usual patter, automatic and mindless. Then he put his older brother on the line.

'Dad? They got this thing in Scouts, like for the Nets' home opener against the Squires? And it's supposed to be a father–son deal, you know? They're getting the tickets through the troop, so everybody'll be sitting together.'

'And you and Mickey would like to go?'

'Well, could we? Me and Mick are both Nets fans, and they ought to be good this year.'

'Jennifer and I.'

'Huh?'

'Nothing.'

'The only thing, it's kind of expensive.'

'How much is it?'

'Well, it's fifteen dollars a person, but that includes the dinner first and the bus ride out to the Coliseum.'

'How much extra do you have to pay if you don't have the dinner?'

'Huh? I don't – *oh*.' He started to giggle. 'Hey, that's really neat,' he said. 'Let me tell Mick. Dad wants to know how much extra you have to pay if you don't have the dinner. Don't you get it, stupid? Dad? How much extra if you don't ride on the bus?'

'That's the idea.'

'I bet the dinner's chicken *à la king*.'

'It's always chicken *à la king*. Look, the cost's no problem, and if the seats are halfway decent it doesn't sound like too bad a deal. When is it?'

'Well, it's a week from tomorrow. Friday night.'

'That could be a problem. It's pretty short notice.'

'They just told us at the last meeting. Can't we go?'

'I don't know. I've got a case and I don't know how long it'll run. Or if I can steal a few hours in the middle of it.'

'I guess it's a pretty important case, huh?'

'The guy I'm trying to help is charged with murder.'

'Did he do it?'

'I don't think so, but that's not the same as knowing how to prove it.'

'Can't the police investigate and work it out?'

Not when they don't want to, I thought. I said, 'Well, they think my friend is guilty and they're not bothering to look any further. That's why he has me working for him.' I rubbed my temple where a pulse was starting to throb. 'Look, here's how we'll do it. Why don't you go ahead and make the arrangements, all right? I'm sending your mother some money tomorrow and I'll send an extra forty-five bucks for the tickets. If I can't make it I'll let you know and you can just give one ticket away and tag along with somebody else. How does that sound?'

There was a pause. 'The thing is, Jack said he would take us if you couldn't.'

'Jack?'

'He's Mom's friend.'

'Uh-huh.'

'But you know, it's supposed to be a father–son thing, and he's not our father.'

'Right. Hang on a second, will you?' I didn't actually need a drink, but I couldn't see how it would hurt me.

I capped the bottle and said, 'How do you get along with Jack?'

'Oh, he's okay.'

'That's good. Well, see how this sounds. I'll take you if I possibly can. If not, you can use my ticket and take Jack. Okay?'

That's how we left it.

In Armstrong's I nodded to four or five people but didn't find the man I was looking for. I sat down at my table. When Trina came over I asked her if Doug Fuhrmann had been in.

'You're an hour late,' she said. 'He dropped in, drank one beer, cashed a check and split.'

'Do you happen to know where he lives?'

She shook her head. 'In the neighborhood, but I couldn't tell you where. Why?'

'I wanted to get in touch with him.'

'I'll ask Don.'

But Don didn't know either. I had a bowl of pea soup and a hamburger. When Trina brought my coffee she sat down across from me and rested her little pointed chin on the back of her hand. 'You're in a funny mood,' she said.

'I'm always in a funny mood.'

'Funny for you, I mean. Either you're working or you're uptight about something.'

'Maybe both.'

'Are you working?'

'Uh-huh.'

'Is that why you're looking for Doug Fuhrmann? Are you working for him?'

'For a friend of his.'

'Did you try the telephone book?'

I touched my index finger to the tip of her little nose. 'You ought to be a detective,' I said. 'Probably do a lot better at it than me.'

Except that he wasn't in the book.

There were around two dozen Fuhrmanns in the Manhattan directory, twice that number of Furmans, and a handful of Fermans and Fermins. I established all this closeted in my hotel room with a phone book, and then I placed my calls from the booth downstairs, stopping periodically to get more dimes from Vinnie. Calls from my room cost double and it's annoying enough to waste dimes to no purpose. I tried all the Fuhrmanns, however spelled, within a two-mile radius of Armstrong's, and I talked to a lot of people with the same last name as my writer friend and a few with the same first name as well, but I didn't reach anybody who knew him and it took a lot of dimes before I gave up.

I went back to Armstrong's around eleven, maybe a little later. A couple of nurses had my regular table so I took one over on the side. I gave the bar crowd a fast glance just to make sure Fuhrmann wasn't there, and then Trina scurried over and said, 'Don't look or anything, but there's somebody at the bar who's been asking about you.'

'I didn't know you could talk without moving your lips.'

'About three stools from the front. Big guy, he was wearing a hat, but I don't know if he still is.'

'He is.'

'You know him?'

'You could always quit this grind and become a ventriloquist,' I suggested. 'Or you could act in one of those old prison movies. If they still make them. He can't read your lips, kid. You've got your back to him.'

'Do you know who he is?'

'Uh-huh. It's all right.'

'Should I tell him you're here?'

'You don't have to. He's on his way over here. Find out what he's drinking from Don and bring him a refill. And I'll have my usual.'

I watched as Eddie Koehler came over, pulled a chair back, settled himself on it. We looked at each other, careful appraising looks. He took a cigar from his jacket pocket and unwrapped it, then patted his pockets until he found a toothpick to puncture its end. He spent a lot of time lighting the cigar, turning it in the flame to get it burning evenly.

We still hadn't spoken when Trina came back with the drinks. His looked to be scotch and water. She asked if he wanted it mixed and he nodded. She mixed it and put it on the table in front of him, then served me my cup of coffee and my double shot of bourbon. I took a short sip of the bourbon neat and poured the rest of it into my coffee.

Eddie said, 'You're tough to get hold of. I left you a couple of messages. I guess you never got over to your hotel to pick'em up.'

'I picked them up.'

'Yeah, that's what the clerk said earlier when I checked. So I guess my line must of been busy when you tried to call me.'

'I didn't call.'

'That so?'

'I had things to do, Eddie.'

'No time to call an old friend, huh?'

'I figured to call you in the morning.'

'Uh-huh.'

'Sometime tomorrow, anyway.'

'Uh-huh. Tonight you were busy.'

'That's right.'

He seemed to notice his drink for the first time. He looked at it as if it was the first one he had ever seen. He switched his cigar to his left hand and lifted the glass with his right. He sniffed it and looked at me. 'Smells like what I been drinking,' he said.

'I told her to bring you another of the same.'

'It's nothing fancy. Seagram's. Same as I been drinking for years.'

'That's right, that's what you always used to have.'

He nodded. ''Course, it's rare for me to have more'n two, three in a day. Two, three drinks – I guess that's just about what you have for breakfast, huh, Matt?'

'Oh, it's not quite that bad, Eddie.'

'No? Glad to hear it. You hear things around, you know. Be amazed what you hear around.'

'I can imagine.'

'Sure you can. Well, what do you want to drink to, anyhow? Any special toast?'

'Nothing special.'

'Speaking of special, how about the Special Prosecutor? You got any objection to drinking to Mr Abner L. Prejanian?'

'Whatever you say.'

'Fine.' He raised his glass. 'To Prejanian, may he drop dead and may he rot.'

I touched my cup to his glass and we drank.

'You got no objection to drinking that toast, huh?'

I shrugged. 'Not if it makes you happy. I don't know the man we're drinking to.'

'You never met the son of a bitch?'

'No.'

'I did. Greasy little cocksucker.' He took another sip of his drink, then shook his head with annoyance and put his glass on the table. 'Aw, fuck this, Matt. How long we known each other?'

'It's been a few years, Eddie.'

'I guess it has. What the fuck are you doing with a shithead like Broadfield, will you tell me that? What the fuck are you doing playing games with him?'

'He hired me.'

'To do what?'

'Find evidence that will clear him.'

'Find a way for him to beat a murder charge, that's what he wants you to do. Do you know what a son of a bitch he is? Do you have any fucking idea?'

'I have a pretty good idea.'

'He's gonna try to give the entire department the shaft, that's all he's trying to do. He's gonna help that shitkicker of a rug peddler expose corruption in high places. Christ, I hate that candyass son of a bitch. He was as corrupt a cop as you'd ever want to see. I mean he went out hunting for it, Matt. Not just taking everything they handed him. He hunted it. He would go out and detect like crazy, looking for crap games and smack dealers and everything else. But not to arrest them. Only if they weren't holding money, then they might make the trip to the station house. But he was in business for himself. His badge was a license to steal.'

'I know all that.'

'You know all that and yet you're working for him.'

'What if he didn't kill the girl, Eddie?'

'She was stone dead in his apartment.'

'And you think he's stupid enough to kill her and leave her there?'

'Oh, shit.' He puffed on his cigar and the end glowed red. 'He got out of there and dumped the murder weapons. Whatever he hit her with and whatever he stabbed her with. Say he went down to the river and dumped them. Then he stopped somewhere to have a couple of beers because he's a cocky son of a bitch and he's a little bit crazy. Then he came back for the body. He was going to dump her someplace but by then we got men on the scene and they're laying for him.'

'So he walked right into their arms.'

'So?'

I shook my head. 'It doesn't make sense. He may be a little crazy but he's certainly not stupid and you're arguing that he acted like an idiot. How did your boys know to go to that apartment in the first place? The papers said you got a telephone tip. Is that right?'

'It's right.'

'Anonymous?'

'Yeah. So?'

'That's very handy. Who would know to tip you? Did she scream? Anybody else hear her? Where did the tip come from?'

'What's the difference? Maybe somebody looked in a

window. Whoever called said there was a woman murdered in such-and-such an apartment, and a couple of the boys went there and found a woman with a bump on her head and a knife wound in her back and she was dead. Who cares how the tipster knew she was there?'

'It might make a difference. If he put her there, for instance.'

'Aw, come on, Matt.'

'You don't have any hard evidence. None. It's all circumstantial.'

'It's enough to nail the lid on. We got motive, we got opportunity, we got the woman dead in his goddam apartment, for Christ's sake. What more do you want? He had every reason to kill her. She was nailing his balls to the wall, and of course he wanted her dead.' He swallowed some more of his drink. He said, 'You know, you used to be a hell of a good cop. Maybe the booze is getting to you these days. Maybe it's more than you can handle.'

'Could be.'

'Oh, hell.' He sighed heavily. 'You can take his money, Matt. A guy has to make a living. I know how it is. Just don't get in the way, huh? Take his money and string him for all he's worth. The hell, he's been on the other end of it often enough. Let him get played for a sucker for a change.'

'I don't think he killed her.'

'Shit.' He took his cigar out of his mouth and stared at it, then clamped his teeth around it and puffed on it. Then, his tone softer, he said, 'You know, Matt, the department's pretty clean these days. Cleaner than it's been in years. Almost all of the old-style pads have been eliminated. There's still some people taking big money, no question about it, but the old system with money delivered by a bagman and distributed through an entire precinct, you don't see that anymore.'

'Even uptown?'

'Well, one of the uptown precincts is probably still a little dirty. It's hard to keep it clean up there. You know how it goes. Aside from that, though, the department stacks up pretty good.'

'So?'

'So we're policing ourselves pretty nicely, and this son of a bitch makes us look like shit all over again, and a lot of good men are going to be up against the wall just because one son of a bitch wants to be an angel and another son of a bitch of a rug peddler wants to be governor.'

'That's why you hate Broadfield but—'

'You're fucking right I hate him.'

'—but why do you want to see him in jail?' I leaned forward. 'He's finished already, Eddie. He's washed up. I talked to one of Prejanian's staff members. They have no use for him. He could get off the hook tomorrow and Prejanian wouldn't dare pick him up. Whoever framed him already did enough of a job on him from your point of view. What's wrong with my going after the killer?'

'We already got the killer. He's in a cell in the Tombs.'

'Let's just suppose you're wrong, Eddie. Then what?'

He stared hard at me. 'All right,' he said. 'Let's suppose I'm wrong. Let's suppose your boy is clean and pure as the snow. Let's say he never did a bad thing in his life. Let's say somebody else killed What's-her-name.'

'Portia Carr.'

'Right. And somebody deliberately framed Broadfield and set him up for a fall.'

'So?'

'And you go after the guy and you get him.'

'So?'

'And he's a cop, because who else would have such a good goddam reason to send Broadfield up?'

'Oh.'

'Yeah, *oh*. That's gonna look terrific, isn't it?' He had his chin jutting at me, and the tendons in his throat were taut. His eyes were furious. 'I don't say that's what happened,' he said. 'Because for my money Broadfield's as guilty as Judas, but if he's not, then somebody did a job on him, and who could it be but a couple of cops who want to give that son of a bitch what he deserves? And that would look beautiful, wouldn't it? A cop kills a girl and pins it on another cop to head off an investigation into police corruption. That would look just beautiful.'

I thought about it. 'And if that's what happened, you'd rather see Broadfield go to jail for something he didn't do than for it to come out in the open. Is that what you're saying?'

'Shit.'

'Is that what you're saying, Eddie?'

'Oh, for Christ's sake. I'd rather see him dead, Matt. Even if I had to blow his fucking head off all by myself.'

93

'Matt? You okay?'

I looked up at Trina. Her apron was off and she had her coat over her arm. 'You leaving?'

'I just finished my shift. You've been putting away a lot of bourbon. I just wondered if you were all right.'

I nodded.

'Who was that man you were talking with?'

'An old friend. He's a cop, a lieutenant working out of the Sixth Precinct. That's down in the Village.' I picked up my glass but put it down again without drinking from it. 'He was about the best friend I had on the force. Not buddy-buddy, but we got along pretty well. Of course, you drift apart over the years.'

'What did he want?'

'He just wanted to talk.'

'You seemed upset after he left.'

I looked up at her. I said, 'The thing is, murder is different. Taking a human life, that's something completely different. Nobody should be allowed to get away with that. Nobody should ever be allowed to get away with that.'

'I don't follow you.'

'He didn't do it, damn it. He didn't, he's innocent, and nobody cares. Eddie Koehler doesn't care. I know Eddie Koehler. He's a good cop.'

'Matt—'

'But he doesn't care. He wants me to coast and not even make an effort because he wants that poor bastard to go to jail for a murder he didn't commit. And he wants the one who really did it to get away with it.'

'I don't think I understand what you're saying, Matt.

Look, don't finish that drink, huh? You don't really need it, do you?'

Everything seemed very clear to me. I couldn't fathom why Trina seemed to be having difficulty following me. I was enunciating clearly enough, and my thoughts, at least to me, flowed with crystalline clarity.

'Crystalline clarity,' I said.

'What?'

'I know what he wants. Nobody else can figure it, but it's obvious. You know what he wants, Diana?'

'I'm Trina, Matt. Honey, don't you know who I am?'

'Of course I do. Slip of the tongue. Don't you know what he wants, baby? He wants the glory.'

'Who does, Matt? The man you were talking to?'

'Eddie?' I laughed at the notion. 'Eddie Koehler doesn't give a damn about glory. I'm talking about Jerry. Good old Jerry.'

'Uh-huh.' She uncurled my fingers from around my glass and lifted the glass free. 'I'll be right back,' she said. 'I won't be a minute, Matt.' And then she went away, and shortly after that she was back again. I may have gone on talking to her while she was away from the table. I'm not too certain one way or the other.

'Let's go home, Matt. I'll walk you home, all right? Or would you like to stay at my place tonight?'

I shook my head. 'Can't do that.'

'Of course you can.'

'No. Have to see Doug Fuhrmann. Very important to see old Doug, baby.'

'Did you find him in the book?'

'That's it. The book. He can put us all in a book, baby. That's where he comes in.'

'I don't understand.'

I frowned, irritated. I was making perfect sense and couldn't understand why my meaning was evidently eluding her. She was a bright girl, Trina was. She ought to be able to understand.

'The check,' I said.

'You already settled your check, Matt. And you tipped me, you gave me too much. Come on, please, stand up, that's an angel. Oh, baby, the world did a job on you, didn't it? It's okay. All the times you helped me get it together, I can do it for you once in a while, can't I?'

'The check, Trina.'

'You paid the check, I just told you, and—'

'Fuhrmann's check.' It was easier to talk clearly now, easier to think more clearly, standing on my feet. 'He cashed a check here earlier tonight. That's what you said.'

'So?'

'Check would be in the register, wouldn't it?'

'Sure. So what? Look, Matt, let's get out in the fresh air and you'll feel a lot better.'

I held up a hand. 'I'm all right,' I insisted. 'Fuhrmann's check's in the register. Ask Don if you can have a look at it.' She still didn't follow me. 'His address,' I explained. 'Most people have their address printed on their checks. I should have thought of it before. Go see, will you? Please?'

And the check was in the register and it had his address on it. She came back and read off the address to me. I gave her my notebook and pen and told her to write it down for me.

'But you can't go there now, Matt. It's too late and you're not up to it.'

'It's too late, and I'm too drunk.'

'In the morning—'

'I don't usually get so drunk, Trina. But I'm all right.'

'Of course you are, baby. Let's get out in the air. See? It's better already. That's the baby.'

EIGHT

It was a hard morning. I swallowed some aspirin and went downstairs to the Red Flame for a lot of coffee. It helped a little. My hands were slightly shaky and my stomach kept threatening to turn over.

What I wanted was a drink. But I wanted it badly enough to know not to have it. I had things to do, places to go, people to see. So I stuck with the coffee.

At the Post Office on Sixtieth Street I purchased a money order for a thousand dollars and another for forty-five dollars. I addressed an envelope and mailed them both to Anita. Then I walked around the corner to St Paul's on Ninth Avenue. I must have sat there for fifteen or twenty minutes, not thinking of anything in particular. On the way out I stopped in front of the effigy of St Anthony and lit a couple of candles for some absent friends. One was for Portia Carr, another for Estrellita Rivera, a couple others for a couple of other people. Then I put five fifty-dollar bills in the slot of the poor box and went out into the cold morning air.

I have an odd relationship with churches, and it's one I do not entirely understand myself. It started not long after I moved to my Fifty-seventh Street hotel. I began spending time in churches, and I began lighting candles, and, ultimately, I began tithing. That last is the most curious part of all. I give a tenth of whatever money I make to the first church I happen to stop in after I receive payment. I don't know what they do with the money. They probably spend half of it converting happy pagans and use the rest to buy large cars for the clergy. But I keep giving my money to them and go on wondering why.

The Catholics get most of my money because of the hours they keep. Their churches are more often open. Otherwise I'm as ecumenical as you can get. A tenth of Broadfield's first payment to me had gone to St Bartholomew's, an Episcopal church in Portia Carr's neighborhood, and now a tenth of his second payment went to St Paul's.

God knows why.

Doug Fuhrmann lived on Ninth Avenue between Fifty-third and Fifty-fourth. To the left of the ground-floor hardware store there was a doorway with a sign over it announcing the availability of furnished rooms by week or month. There were no mailboxes in the vestibule and no individual buzzers. I rang the bell alongside the inner door and waited until a woman with henna-bright hair shuffled to the door and opened it. She wore a plaid robe and had shabby bedroom slippers on her feet. 'Full up,' she said. 'Try three doors down, he's usually got something available.'

I told her I was looking for Douglas Fuhrmann.

'Fourth floor front,' she said. 'He expecting you?'

'Yes.' Although he wasn't.

''Cause he usually sleeps late. You can go on up.'

I climbed three flights of stairs, making my way through the sour smells of a building that had given up along with its tenants. I was surprised that Fuhrmann lived in a place like this. Men who live in broken-down Hell's Kitchen rooming houses don't usually have their addresses printed on their checks. They don't usually have checking accounts.

I stood in front of his door. A radio was playing, and then I heard a burst of very rapid typing, then nothing but the radio. I knocked on the door. I heard the sound of a chair being pushed back, and then Fuhrmann's voice asked who it was.

'Scudder.'

'Matt? Just a second.' I waited and the door opened and Fuhrmann gave me a big smile. 'Come on in,' he said. 'Jesus, you look like hell. You got a cold or something?'

'I had a hard night.'

'Want some coffee? I can give you a cup of instant. How'd you find me, anyway? Or is that a professional secret? I guess detectives have to be good at finding people.'

He scurried around, plugged in an electric tea kettle, measured instant coffee into a pair of white china cups. He kept up a steady stream of conversation, but I wasn't listening to him. I was busy looking over the place where he lived.

I hadn't been prepared for it. It was just one room, but it was a large one, measuring perhaps eighteen by twenty-five feet, with two windows overlooking Ninth Avenue. What made it remarkable was the dramatic contrast between it and the building it was situated in. All of the drabness and decay stopped at Fuhrmann's threshold.

He had a rug on the floor, either an authentic Persian

or a convincing imitation. His walls were lined with floor-to-ceiling, built-in bookshelves. A desk a full twelve feet in length extended in front of the windows. It too had been built in. Even the paint on the walls was distinctive, the walls themselves – where they were not covered with bookshelves – painted in a dark ivory, the trim set off in a glossy white enamel.

He saw me taking it all in, and his eyes danced behind his thick glasses. 'That's how everybody reacts,' he said. 'You climb those stairs and it's depressing, right? And then you walk into my little retreat and it's almost shocking.' The kettle whistled and he made our coffee. 'It's not as though I planned it this way,' he said. 'I took this place a dozen years ago because I could afford it and there wasn't much else I could afford. I was paying fourteen dollars a week. And I'll tell you something, there were weeks when it was a struggle to come up with the fourteen bucks.'

He stirred the coffee, passed my cup to me. 'Then I got so I was making a living, but even so, I was a little hesitant about moving. I like the location, the sense of neighborhood. I even like the *name* of the neighborhood. *Hell's Kitchen.* If you're going to be a writer, where better to live than a place called Hell's Kitchen? Besides, I didn't want to commit myself to a big rent. I was getting ghostwriting assignments, I was building up a list of magazine editors who knew my work, but even so, it's not a steady business and I didn't want to have a big monthly nut to crack. So what I did, I started fixing this place up and making it bearable. I'd do a little at a time. First thing I did was put in a full burglar alarm system because I got really paranoid about the idea of some junkie kicking the door in and ripping off my typewriter. Then the bookshelves because I was tired of having all my books piled up in cartons. And then the desk, and then I got rid of the original bed, which I think George Washington must have slept in, and I bought that platform bed which sleeps eight in a pinch, and little by little the whole place came together. I kind of like it. I don't think I'm ever going to move.'

'It suits you, Doug.'

He nodded eagerly. 'Yeah, I think it does. A couple of years ago I started to twitch because it occurred to me that they could boot me out. Here I got a ton invested in the place and what do I do if they raise my rent? I mean I was still paying by the week, for Christ's sake. The rent was up, it was maybe twenty bucks, but suppose they raise it to a hundred a week? Who knows what they're gonna do, you know? So what I did, I told'em I'd pay a hundred and twenty-five a month, and on top of that I'd give them five hundred in cash under the table. For that I wanted a thirty-year lease.'

'And they gave it to you?'

'You ever heard of anybody with a thirty-year lease on a room on Ninth Avenue? They thought they had a real idiot on their hands.' He chuckled. 'On top of which they never rented a room for more than twenty a week, and I was offering thirty plus cash under the table. They drew up a lease and I signed it. You know what people pay for a studio apartment this size and this location?'

'Now? Two-fifty, three hundred.'

'Three hundred easy. I still pay one and a quarter. In another two or three years this place'll be worth five hundred a month, maybe a thousand if the inflation keeps up. And I'll *still* pay one and a quarter. There's a guy buying up property all up and down Ninth Avenue. Someday they're going to start knocking down these buildings like tenpins. But they'll have to either buy up my lease from me or wait until the lease runs out to knock the building down. Beautiful?'

'You got a good deal, Doug.'

'Only clever thing I ever did in my life, Matt. And I wasn't looking to be clever. It's just I'm comfortable here and I hate moving.'

I took a sip of my coffee. It wasn't much worse than what I'd had for breakfast. I said, 'How did you and Broadfield get to be such buddies?'

'Yeah, I figured that's why you were here. Is he crazy or something? Why did he go and kill her? There's no point to it at all.'

'I know it.'

'He always struck me as an even-tempered guy. Men that size have to be steady or they do too much damage. A guy like me could have a short fuse and it wouldn't matter because I'd need a cannon to do any damage, but Broadfield – I guess he blew up and killed her, huh?'

I shook my head. 'Somebody knocked her over the head and then stuck a knife into her. You don't do that on an impulse.'

'The way you said it, you sound as though you don't think he did it.'

'I'm sure he didn't.'

'Jesus, I hope you're right.'

I looked at him. The large forehead and the thick

glasses gave him the look of an extremely intelligent insect. I said, 'Doug, how do you know him?'

'An article I was doing once. I had to talk to some cops for research, and he was one of the ones I talked to. We hit it off pretty well.'

'When was that?'

'Maybe four, five years ago. Why?'

'And you're just friends? And that's why he decided to turn to you when he was on the spot?'

'Well, I don't think he *has* too many friends, Matt. And he couldn't turn to any cop friends of his. He told me once that cops don't usually have many friends off the force.'

That was true enough. But Broadfield didn't seem to have many friends *on* the force, either.

'Why did he go to Prejanian in the first place, Doug?'

'Hell, don't ask me. Ask Broadfield.'

'But you know the answer, don't you?'

'Matt—'

'He wants to write a book. That's it, isn't it? He wants to make a big enough splash to be a celebrity, and he wants you to write his book for him. And then he can do all the television talk shows and grin that cute grin of his and call a lot of important people by their first names. That's where you come into it. That's the only way you can come into it, and it's the only reason that would have sent him to Abner Prejanian's office.'

He wouldn't look at me. 'He wanted it a secret, Matt.'

'Sure. And afterward he would just happen to write a book. In response to popular demand.'

'It could be dynamite. Not just his role with the investigation but his whole life. He's told me the most fascinating stuff I've ever heard. I wish he'd let me tape some of it, but so far everything's off the record. When I heard he killed her I saw the chance of my life going down the drain. But if he's really innocent—'

'Where did he get the idea of doing the book?'

He hesitated, then shrugged. 'You might as well know it all. It's a natural idea, cop books are big these days, but he might not have thought of it by himself.'

'Portia Carr.'

'That's right, Matt.'

'She suggested it? No, that doesn't make sense.'

'She was talking about doing a book herself.'

I put my cup down and went over to the window. 'What kind of a book?'

'I don't know. Something like *The Happy Hooker*, I suppose. What's the difference?'

'Hardesty.'

'Huh?'

'I'll bet that's why he went to Hardesty.'

He looked at me.

'Knox Hardesty,' I said. 'The U.S. District Attorney. Broadfield went to him before he went to Prejanian, and when I asked him why he didn't make much sense. Because Prejanian was the logical man to go to. Police corruption is his special area of interest, and it wouldn't carry much weight with a federal D.A.'

'So?'

'So Broadfield would have known that. He only would have picked Hardesty if he thought he had some kind of an in there. He probably got the idea of writing a book from Portia Carr. Maybe he got the idea of Hardesty from the same place.'

'What does Portia Carr have to do with Knox Hardesty?'

I told him it was a good question.

NINE

Hardesty's offices were at 26 Federal Plaza with the rest of the Justice Department's New York operations. That put him just a couple of blocks from Abner Prejanian; I wondered if Broadfield had dropped in on both of them the same day.

I called first, to make sure Hardesty wasn't in court or out of town. He was neither, but I saved myself a trip downtown because his secretary told me he hadn't come in, that he was home with stomach flu. I asked for his home address and telephone number, but she wasn't allowed to give them to me.

The telephone company wasn't similarly restricted. He was listed. *Hardesty, Knox, 114 East End Avenue*, and a phone number with a Regent 4 exchange. I called the number and got through to Hardesty. He sounded as though stomach flu had been a polite term for hangover. I told him my name and that I wanted to see him. He said he didn't feel well and started to hedge, and the only decent card I had was Portia Carr's name, so I played it.

I'm not sure exactly what reaction I expected, but it certainly wasn't the one I got. 'Poor Portia. That was a tragic thing, wasn't it? You were a friend of hers, Scudder? Be very anxious to get together with you. Wouldn't happen to be free right now, I don't suppose.

You would? Good, very good. You know the address here?'

I figured it out in the cab on the way over there. I'd somehow managed to take it for granted that Hardesty had been one of Portia's clients, and I'd envisioned him hopping around in a tutu while she flailed at him with a whip. And men in public office with political ambitions don't usually welcome inquiries on their unorthodox sexual practices from total strangers. I'd expected outright denial that he knew Portia Carr ever existed, or some hedging at the very least. Instead I got a very eager welcome.

So I'd obviously added things wrong. The list of Portia's prominent clients didn't include Knox Hardesty. Theirs was a professional relationship, no doubt, but it was his profession that was involved, not hers.

And that way it made plenty of sense. And it fit in with Portia's literary aspirations and connected neatly to Broadfield's ambitions in that direction.

Hardesty's building was a prewar stonefront fourteen stories tall. It had an Art Deco Lobby with high ceilings and a lot of black marble. The doorman had auburn hair and a guardsman's moustache. He established that I was expected and passed me on to the elevator operator, a diminutive black who was barely tall enough to reach the top button. And he had to reach it because Hardesty had the penthouse.

And the penthouse was impressive. High ceilings, rich, high-pile carpet, fireplaces, oriental antiques. A Jamaican maid led me into the study where Hardesty was waiting for me. He stood up and came out from behind his desk, his hand extended. We shook hands and he waved me to a chair.

'A drink? A cup of coffee? I'm drinking milk myself because of this damned ulcer. I picked up a touch of stomach flu and it always aggravates the ulcer. But what will you have, Scudder?'

'Coffee, if it's no trouble. Black.'

Hardesty repeated the order to the maid as if she couldn't have been expected to follow our conversation. She returned almost immediately with a mirrored tray holding a silver pot of coffee, a bone-china cup and saucer, a silver cream and sugar set, and a spoon. I poured out a cup of coffee and took a sip.

'So you knew Portia,' Hardesty said. He drank some milk, put the glass down. He was tall and thin, his hair graying magnificently at his temples, his summertime tan not entirely faded yet. I'd been able to picture what a striking couple Broadfield and Portia must have made. She would have looked good on Knox Hardesty's arm, too.

'I didn't know her terribly well,' I said. 'But I knew her, yes.'

'Yes. Hmmm. I don't believe I asked you your profession, Scudder.'

'I'm a private detective.'

'Oh, very interesting. Very interesting. Is that coffee all right, incidentally?'

'It's the best I've ever tasted.'

He allowed himself a smile. 'My wife's the coffee fanatic. I was never that much of an enthusiast, and with the ulcer I tend to stick to milk.

I could find out the brand for you if you're interested.'

'I live in a hotel, Mr Hardesty. When I want coffee I go around the corner for it. But thank you.'

'Well, you can always drop in here for a decent cup of the stuff, can't you?' He gave me a nice rich smile. Knox Hardesty didn't live on his salary as United States Attorney for the Southern District of New York. That wouldn't cover his rent. But that didn't mean he walked around with his hand out. Grandfather Hardesty had owned Hardesty Iron and Steel before U.S. Steel bought him up, and Grandfather Knox had followed a long line of New England Knoxes in shipping. Knox Hardesty could spend money with both hands and still never have to worry where his next glass of milk was coming from.

He said, 'A private detective, and you were acquainted with Portia. You could be very useful to me, Mr Scudder.'

'I was hoping things might work the other way around.'

'I beg your pardon?' His face changed and his back stiffened and he looked as though he had just smelled something extremely unpleasant. I guess my line had sounded like the overture of a blackmail pitch.

'I already have a client,' I said. 'I came to you to find something out, not to give information away. Or even to sell it, as far as that goes. And I'm not a blackmailer, sir. I wouldn't want to give that impression.'

'You have a client?'

I nodded. I was just as glad I'd given the impression I did, although it had been unintentional on my part. His reaction had been unequivocal enough. If I was a blackmailer he wanted no part of me. And that generally means the person in question doesn't have reason to fear being blackmailed. Whatever his relationship with Portia, it wasn't something he would have trouble living down.

'I'm representing Jerome Broadfield.'

'The man who killed her.'

'The police think so, Mr Hardesty. Then again, you'd expect them to think so, wouldn't you?'

'Good point. I'd been given to understand he was virtually caught in the act. That's not the case?' I shook my head. 'Interesting. And you'd like to find out—'

'I'd like to find out who killed Miss Carr and framed my client.'

He nodded. 'But I don't see how I can help you toward that end, Mr Scudder.'

I'd been promoted – from Scudder to Mr Scudder. I said, 'How did you happen to know Portia Carr?'

'One has to know a wide variety of people in my line of work. The most fruitful contacts are not necessarily those persons with whom one would prefer to associate. I'm sure that has been your own experience as well, hasn't it? One sort of investigative work is rather like another, I suspect.' He smiled graciously; I was supposed to be complimented that he saw his work as being similar to mine.

'I heard of Miss Carr before I met her,' he went on. 'The better sort of prostitutes can be very useful to our office. I was informed that Miss Carr was quite expensive and that her client list was primarily interested in, oh, less orthodox forms of sex.'

'I understand she specialized in masochists.'

'Quite.' He made a face; he'd have preferred it if I'd been less specific. 'English, you know. That's the English vice, so-called, and an American masochist would find an English mistress especially desirable. Or so Miss Carr informed me. Did you know that native-born prostitutes oft-times affect English or German accents for the benefit of their masochistic clients? Miss Carr assured me it's common practice. German accents for the Jewish clients in particular, which I find fascinating.'

I freshened my cup of coffee.

'The fact that Miss Carr's accent was quite authentic increased my interest in her. She was vulnerable, you see.'

'Because she could be deported.'

He nodded. 'We have a good enough working relationship with the fellows in Immigration and Naturalization. Not that it's often necessary to follow through on one's threats. The prostitute's traditional tight-lipped loyalty to her clientele is as much a romantic conceit as her heart of gold. The merest threat of deportation is enough to bring immediate offers of full cooperation.'

'And that was the case with Portia Carr?'

'Absolutely. In fact she became quite eager. I think she relished the Mata Hari role, garnering information in bed and passing it on to me. Not that she managed to supply me with terribly much, but she was shaping up as a promising source for my investigations.'

'Any investigation in particular?'

There was just a little hesitation. 'Nothing specific,' he said. 'I could just see that she would be useful.'

I drank some more coffee. If nothing else, Hardesty was enabling me to find out just how much my own client knew. Since Broadfield had chosen to play coy with me, I had to get this information in an indirect fashion. But Hardesty didn't know that Broadfield hadn't been completely straight with me, so he couldn't deny anything that I might have presumably learned from him.

'So she cooperated enthusiatically,' I said.

'Oh, very much so.' He smiled in reminiscence. 'She was quite charming, you know. And she had the notion of writing a book about her life as a prostitute and her work for me. I think that Dutch girl was an inspiration to her. Of course the Dutch girl can't set foot in the country because of the role she played, but I don't really think Portia Carr would have ever gotten round to writing that book, do you?'

'I don't know. She won't now.'

'No, of course not.'

'Jerry Broadfield might, though. Was he terribly disappointed when you told him you weren't interested in police corruption?'

'I'm not sure I put it quite that way.' He frowned abruptly. 'Is that why he came to me? For heaven's sake. He wanted to write a book?' He shook his head in disbelief. 'I'll never understand people,' he said. 'I knew that self-righteousness was a pose, and that made me resolve not to have anything to do with him, that more than the sort of information he had to offer. I simply couldn't trust him and felt he'd do my investigations

113

more harm than good. So then he popped over to see that Special Prosecutor chap.'

That Special Prosecutor chap. It wasn't hard to tell what Knox Hardesty thought of Abner L. Prejanian.

I said, 'Did it bother you that he went to Prejanian?'

'Why on earth should it bother me?'

I shrugged. 'Prejanian started to get a lot of ink. The papers gave him a nice play.'

'More power to him if publicity is what he wants. It seems rather to have backfired on him now, though. Wouldn't you say?'

'And that must please you.'

'It confirms my judgment, but aside from that why should it please me?'

'Well, you and Prejanian are rivals, aren't you?'

'Oh, I'd hardly put it that way.'

'No? I thought you were. I figured that's why you got her to accuse Broadfield of extortion.'

'What!'

'Why else would you do it?' I made my tone deliberately offhand, not accusing him but taking it for granted that it was something we both knew and acknowledged. 'Once she was pressing charges against him he was defused and Prejanian didn't even hear his name mentioned. And it made Prejanian look gullible for having used Broadfield in the first place.'

His grandfather or great-grandfather might have lost control. But Hardesty had enough generations of good breeding behind him so that he was able to keep almost all of his cool. He straightened in his chair, but that was about the extent of it. 'You've been misinformed,' he told me.

'The charge wasn't Portia's idea.'

'Nor was it mine.'

'Then why did she call you around noon the day before yesterday? She wanted your advice, and you told her to go on acting as if the charge was true. Why did she call you? And why did you tell her that?'

No indignation this time. A little stalling – picking up the glass of milk, putting it down untasted, fussing with a paperweight and a letter opener. Then he looked at me and asked how I knew she'd called him.

'I was there.'

'You were—' His eyes widened. 'You were the man who wanted to talk with her. But I thought – then you were working for Broadfield *before* the murder.'

'Yes.'

'For heaven's sake. I thought – well, obviously I thought you'd been engaged after he was arrested for homicide. Hmmm. So you were the man she was so nervous about. But I spoke to her before she had met you. She didn't even know your name when we talked. How did you know – she didn't tell you, that's the last thing she would have done. Oh, for heaven's sake. That was a bluff, wasn't it?'

'You could call it an educated guess.'

'I'd just as soon call it a bluff. I'm not sure I'd care to play poker with you, Mr Scudder. Yes, she called me – I might as well admit it since it's fairly obvious. And I told her to insist that the charge was true, although I knew it wasn't. But I didn't put her up to making the charge in the first place.'

'Then who did?'

'Some policemen. I don't know their names, and I'm

not inclined to think Miss Carr did. She said she didn't, and it's likely she'd have been open with me on that subject. You see, she hadn't wanted to press those charges. If there was a chance I could have gotten her off that hook, she'd have done what she could.' He smiled. 'You may think I had reason to cast a pall on Mr Prejanian's investigation. While I'm not saddened by the spectacle of that man with egg on his face, I'd never have taken the trouble to put it there. Certain policemen, however, had a much stronger motive for sabotaging that inquiry.'

'What did they have on Carr?'

'I don't know. Prostitutes are always vulnerable, of course, but—'

'Yes?'

'Oh, this is just intuitive on my part. I had the impression that they were threatening her not with the law but with some extralegal punishment. I believe she was physically afraid of them.'

I nodded. That checked out with the vibrations I'd picked up at my own meeting with Portia Carr. She hadn't acted like someone afraid of deportation or arrest, but like someone worried about being beaten up or killed. Someone worried because it was October and she was waiting for winter.

TEN

Elaine lived just three blocks from where Portia Carr had lived. Her building was on Fifty-first between First and Second. The doorman checked me on the intercom and motioned me on through. By the time the elevator got me to the ninth floor, Elaine was waiting in her open doorway.

I decided she looked a lot better than Prejanian's secretary. I suppose she's around thirty by now. She has always looked younger than her years and she has a face full of good bones that will age well. Her softness contrasted dramatically with the stark, modern feel of her apartment. She had the place carpeted in white shag, and the furniture was all angles and geometric planes and primary colors. I don't ordinarily like rooms done that way, but somehow her place worked for me. She'd told me once that she had done her own decorating.

We kissed each other like the old friends we were. Then she gripped my elbows and leaned backward. 'Secret Agent Mardell reporting,' she said. 'I'm not to be taken lightly, man. This camera of mine just looks like a camera. It's actually a tie clip.'

'I think that's backward.'

'Well, I certainly hope so.' She turned, flounced away. 'Actually I haven't found out a hell of a lot. You want to know what prominent people were in her book, is that right?'

'Especially if they're politically prominent.'

'That's what I meant. Everybody I asked kept coming up with the same three or four names. Actors, a couple of musicians. Honestly, some call girls are as bad as groupies. Boasting like any other celebrity-fuckers.'

'You're the second person today to tell me call girls don't keep everything confidential.'

'Ha! Your average hooker isn't exactly Stella Stable, Matt. Of course I'm the winner of the Miss Mental Health contest.'

'Absolutely.'

'If she didn't mention what politicians were in her book, it's probably because she wasn't that proud of them. If she'd been fucking the governor or a U.S. senator, people would have heard about it, but if it's somebody local, who cares? What's the matter?'

'Politicians would probably be sad to learn that they're not so important.'

'They'd positively shit, wouldn't they?' She lit a cigarette. 'What you ought to have is her john book. Even if she had the brains to code it, you'd have the phone numbers and you can work backward from there.'

'Is yours in code?'

'The names *and* the numbers, sugar.' She smiled triumphantly. 'Anybody who steals my book steals trash, just like Othello's purse. But that's because I'm Brenda Brilliant. Could you get your hands on Portia's book?'

I shook my head. 'I'm sure the cops have tossed her

place. And if she had a book, they found it – and tossed it. In the river. They don't want any loose ends that might give Broadfield's lawyer an opening. They want him drawn and quartered, and the only way they'd leave her book around is if Broadfield's name was the only one in it.'

'Who do you figure killed her, Matt? Some cops?'

'People keep suggesting it. Maybe I've been off the force too long. I have trouble believing that police officers would actually murder some innocent hooker just to frame someone else.'

She opened her mouth, then closed it.

'Something?'

'Well, maybe you've been off the force too long.' She looked about to say something else, then gave her head a quick shake. 'I think I'll make myself a cup of tea. I'm a rotten hostess. A drink? I'm out of bourbon, but there's Scotch.'

It was time. 'A small one, straight.'

'Coming right up.'

While she was in the kitchen I thought about the relationship of cops and whores, and the relationship of Elaine and myself. I had gotten to know her a couple of years before I left the police department. Our first meeting was social, though I do not remember the precise circumstances. I believe we were introduced by a mutual friend at some restaurant or other, but we may have met at a party. I don't remember.

It's useful for a hooker to have a cop with whom she's on particularly good terms. He can smooth things out if a brother officer is giving her a hard time. He can furnish her with a brand of reality-oriented legal advice that is often more useful then the advice she would get from a lawyer. And she reciprocates for all of this, of course, as women have always reciprocated for the favors men do for them.

So I spent a couple of years on Elaine Mardell's free list, and I was the person she called when the walls started coming together around her. Neither of us abused the privilege. I would see her once in a while if I happened to be in the neighborhood, and she called me perhaps half a dozen times all told.

Then I left the force, and for a period of several months I wasn't interested in any human contact, least of all sexual contact. Then one day I was, and I called Elaine and went over to see her. She never mentioned that I wasn't a cop any more and that our relationship was thus due to change. If she had, I probably wouldn't have wanted to see her again. But on the way out I put some money on the coffee table, and she said she hoped she'd see me again soon, and every now and then she does.

I suppose our original relationship had constituted a form of police corruption. I hadn't been acting as Elaine's protector, nor had it been my job to arrest her. But I had seen her on the city's time, and it had been my official position that earned me the right to share her bed. Corruption, I suppose.

She brought me my drink, a juice glass with around three ounces of Scotch in it, and sat down on the couch with a cup of tea with milk. She curled her legs under her compact little behind and stirred her tea with a demitasse spoon.

'Beautiful weather,' she said.

'Uh-huh.'

'I wish I was closer to the park. I take long walks every morning. Days like this I'd like to take my walks in the park.'

'You take long walks every morning?'

'Sure. It's good for you. Why?'

'I figured you'd sleep until noon.'

'Oh, no. I'm an early riser. And I'll get visitors from noon on, of course. And I can get to sleep early because it's rare I have anyone here after ten o'clock at night.'

'That's funny. You think of it as a business for night people.'

'Except it's not. The guys, you know, they have to get home to their families. I'd say from noon to six-thirty is maybe ninety percent of the people I see.'

'Makes sense.'

'I got somebody coming in a while, Matt, but we got time if you feel like it.'

'I'd better take a raincheck.'

'Well, that's cool.'

I drank some of my drink. 'Back to Portia Carr,' I said. 'You didn't come up with anybody who might have had some kind of a government connection?'

'Well, I might have.' My face must have changed expression because she said, 'No, I'm not hustling you, for God's sake. I learned a name, but I don't know if I got it right and I don't know who it is.'

'What's the name?'

'Something like Mantz or Manch or Manns. I don't know it exactly. I know he's somebody connected to the mayor, but I don't know what. At least that's the story I got. Don't ask me the guy's first name because nobody knows. Does that give you anything? Manns or Mantz or Manch or something like that?'

'It doesn't ring a bell. He's connected to the mayor?'

'Well, that's what I heard. I know what he likes to do if that helps. He's a toilet slave.'

'What the hell is a toilet slave?'

'I wish you knew because it doesn't especially thrill me to discuss it.' She put her teacup down. 'A toilet slave is, well, they'll have different kinds of kinks, but an example would be that he wants to be ordered to drink piss or eat shit, or to clean out your ass with his tongue, or clean out the toilet, or other things. What you have to tell him to do can be really disgusting or it can just be sort of symbolic, like if you made him mop the bathroom floor.'

'Why would anybody – never mind, don't tell me.'

'It's getting to be a very strange world, Matt.'

'Uh-huh.'

'Like nobody seems to fuck anymore. You can make a ton doing masochist tricks. They'll pay a fortune if you can fill up their fantasy for them. But I don't think it's worth it. I'd rather not have to contend with all that weirdness.'

'You're just an old-fashioned girl, Elaine.'

'That's me. Crinolines and lavender sachets and all those good things. 'Nother drink?'

'Just a touch.'

When she brought it I said, 'Manns or Manch or something like that. I'll see if that goes anywhere. I think it's a dead-end street anyway. I'm getting more and more interested in cops.'

'Because of what I said?'

'That, and also something some other people have said. Did she have somebody on the force that sort of looked out for her?'

'You mean the way you used to for me? Sure she did, but where does that get you? It was your friend.'

'Broadfield?'

'Sure. That extortion number was pure bullshit, but I guess you knew that.'

I nodded. 'She have anybody else?'

'Could be, but I never heard about it. And no pimp and no boyfriends, unless you count Broadfield as a boyfriend.'

'Any other cops in her life? Giving her a hard time, anything like that?'

'Not that I heard about.'

I took a sip of scotch. 'This is off the subject a little, Elaine, but do cops ever give you a hard time?'

'Do you mean do they or have they ever? It's happened in the past. But then I learned a little. You have somebody regular, and the rest of the guys let you be.'

'Sure.'

'And if I get a hard time from somebody else, I mention some names or I make a phone call and everything cools down. You know what's worse? Not cops. Guys pretending to be cops.'

'Impersonating an officer? That's a criminal offense, you know.'

'Well, shit, Matt, am I gonna press charges? Like I've had cats flash badges at me, the whole number. You take a green kid who just got to town and all she's got to see is a silver shield and she'll curl up in a corner and have kittens. I'm supercool myself. I take a good look at the badge and it turns out to be a toy thing that a little kid'll get to go with his cap pistol. Don't laugh, I mean it. I've had that happen.'

'And what do they want from you? Money?'

'Oh, they pretend it's a gag after I pick up on them. But it's no gag. I've had them want money, but mostly all they want is to get fucked for free.'

'And they flash a toy badge.'

'I've seen badges you'd swear came out of cracker-jack boxes.'

'Men are weird animals.'

'Oh, men and women both, honey. I'll tell you something. Everybody's weird, fundamentally every-body is a snap. Sometimes it's a sexual thing and sometimes it's a different kind of weirdness, but one way or another everybody's nuts. You, me, the whole world.'

It wasn't particularly difficult to discover that Leon J. Manch had been appointed assistant deputy mayor a year and a half ago. All it took was a short session in the Forty-second Street library. There were a variety of Mannses and Mantzes in the volume of the *Times Index* I consulted, but none of them seemed to have anything significant to do with the current administration. Manch was mentioned only once in the *Times Indexes* for the past five years. The story dealt with his appointment, and I went to the trouble of reading the article in the microfilm room. It was a brief article, and Manch was one of half a dozen people treated in it; about all it did was announce that he'd been appointed and identify him as a member of the bar. I learned nothing about his age, residence, marital status, or much of anything else. It didn't say he was a toilet slave, but I already knew that.

I couldn't find him in the Manhattan telephone book. Maybe he lived in another borough, or outside of the city limits altogether. Maybe he had an unlisted phone or listed it in his wife's name. I called City Hall and was told that he'd left for the day. I didn't even try for his home number.

I called her from a bar on Madison and Fifty-first called O'Brien's. The bartender's name was Nick, and I knew him because he had worked at Armstrong's a year or so ago. We assured each other that it was a small world, bought each other a few drinks, and then I went to the phone booth in the back and dialed her number. I had to look it up in my notebook.

When she answered I said, 'It's Matthew. Can you talk?'

'Hello. Yes, I can talk. I'm all alone here. My sister and her husband drove in from Bayport and picked up the children this morning. They'll be staying out there for, oh, for a while, anyway. They thought it would be better for the children and easier for me. I didn't really want them to take the kids, but I didn't have the strength to argue, and maybe they're right, maybe it's better this way.'

'You sound a little shaky.'

'Not shaky. Just very drawn, very worn out. Are you all right?'

'I'm fine.'

'I wish you were here.'

'So do I.'

'Oh, dear. I wish I knew how I felt about all of this. It frightens me. Do you know what I mean?'

'Yes.'

'His lawyer called earlier. Have you spoken to him?'

'No. Was he trying to get in touch with me?'

'He didn't seem very interested in you, as a matter of fact. He was very confident about winning in court, and when I said that you were trying to find out who really killed that woman, he seemed – how shall I put it? I got the impression that he believed Jerry was guilty. He intends to get him acquitted, but he doesn't really believe for a minute that he's really innocent.'

'A lot of lawyers are like that, Diana.'

'Like a surgeon who decides it's his job to remove an appendix. Whether there's anything wrong with the appendix or not.'

'I'm not sure it's exactly the same thing, but I know what you mean. I wonder if there's any point in my contacting that lawyer.'

'I don't know. What I was starting to say … Oh, it's silly, and it's hard to say. Matthew? I was disappointed when I picked up the phone and it was the lawyer. Because I was hoping, oh, that it would be you.' Pause. 'Matthew?'

'I'm here.'

'Should I not have said that?'

'No, don't be silly.' I caught my breath. The telephone booth had gotten unbearably warm. I opened the door a little. 'I wanted to call you earlier. I shouldn't be calling now, really. I can't say I've made very much progress.'

'I'm glad you called, anyway. Are you getting anywhere at all?'

'Maybe. Did your husband ever say anything to you about writing a book?'

'Me write a book? I wouldn't know where to start. I used to write poetry. Not very good poetry, I'm afraid.'

'I meant did he say anything about the possibility of him writing a book.'

'Jerry? He doesn't *read* books, let alone *write* them. Why?'

'I'll tell you when I see you. I'm learning things. The question is whether or not they'll fit together into something significant. He didn't do it. I know that much.'

'You're more certain of it than you were yesterday.'

'Yes.' Pause. 'I've been thinking about you.'

'That's good. I think it's good. What sort of thoughts?'

'Curious ones.'

'Good curious or bad curious?'

'Oh, good, I guess.'

'I've been thinking, too.'

ELEVEN

I wound up spending the evening in the Village. I was oddly restless, possessed of an undirected energy that energised me and kept me moving. It was a Friday night, and the better downtown bars were crowded and noisy as they always are on Fridays. I hit the Kettle and Minetta's and Whitey's and McBell's and the San Giorgio and the Lion's Head and the Riviera and other places the names of which I don't remember. But because I couldn't settle in anywhere I wound up having only one drink to a bar and walking off most of the effect of the alcohol between drinks. I kept moving and I kept drifting west, away from the tourist area and closer to where the Village rubs up against the Hudson River.

It must have been around midnight when I hit Sinthia's. It was fairly far west on Christopher Street, the last stop for gay cruisers on their way to meet the longshoremen and truckers in the shadow of the docks. Gay bars do not threaten me, but neither are they places I habitually seek out. I sometimes dropped in to Sinthias's when I was in the neighborhood because I know the owner fairly well. Fifteen years back I'd had to arrest him for contributing to the delinquency of a minor. The minor in question had been seventeen and jaded, and I'd only made the collar because I'd had no choice – the boy's father had lodged a formal complaint. Kenny's lawyer had a quiet talk with the boy's father and gave him an idea what he would bring out in open court, and that was the end of that.

Over the years Kenny and I had developed a relationship somewhere in the uncertain ground between acquaintance and friendship. He was behind the bar when I walked in, and as always he looked a young twenty-eight years old. His real age must be just about double that, and you have to stand very close to him to spot the face-lift scars. And the carefully combed hair is all Kenny's own, even if the blond color is a gift from a lady named Clairol.

He had around fifteen customers. Seeing them one at a time you'd have no cause to suspect they were gay, but collectively their homosexuality became unmistakable, almost a presence in the long narrow room. Perhaps it was their reaction to my intrusion that was palpable. People who spend their lives in any sort of half-world can always recognize a cop, and I still haven't learned how to avoid looking like one.

'Sir Matthew of Scudder,' Kenny sang out. 'Welcome, welcome as always. The trade around here is rarely quite so rough as your estimable self. Still bourbon, darling? Still heat?'

'Fine, Kenny.'

'I'm glad to see nothing changes. You are a constant in a madcap world.'

I took a seat at the bar. The other drinkers had relaxed when Kenny hailed me, which may well be what he'd had in mind in making such a production out of it. He poured quite a lot of bourbon into a glass and set it on the bar in front of me. I drank some of it. Kenny leaned toward me, propping himself up on his elbows. His face was deeply tanned. He spends his summers on Fire Island and uses a sunlamp the rest of the year.

'Working, sweets?'

'Yes, as a matter of fact.'

He sighed. 'It happens to the best of us. I've been back in harness since Labor Day and I'm still not used to it. Such a joy lying in the sun all summer and leaving this place for Alfred to mismanage. You know Alfred?'

'No.'

'I'm certain he stole me blind and I don't even care. I only kept the place open to accommodate my trade. Not out of the goodness of my heart, but because I don't want these girls to find out there are other establishments in the city that sell liquor. So as long as I covered my overhead I was blissfully happy. And then I wound up showing a slight profit, which was nothing but gravy.' He winked, then scuttled the length of the bar to replenish some drinks and collect some money. Then he returned and posed once again with his chin cupped in his two hands.

He said, 'Bet I know what you're up to.'

'Bet you don't.'

'For a drink? You're on. Let me see now – its initials wouldn't just happen to be J. B. by any chance, would it? And I don't mean the Jim Beam you're drinking. J. B. and his good friend P. C.?' His eyebrows ascended dramatically. 'Heavens, why is your poor jaw plummeting halfway to the dusty floor, Matthew? Isn't that what drew you to this den of ubiquity in the first place?'

I shook my head.

'Really?'

'I just happened to be in the neighborhood.'

'That's quite remarkable.'

'I know he was living just a few blocks from here, but why does that tie him to this place, Kenny? There are dozens of bars as close to his apartment on Barrow. Were you just guessing that I was on his case, or did you hear something?'

'I don't know if you'd call it a guess. More an assumption. He used to drink here.'

'Broadfield?'

'The very same. Not all that often, but every once in a while. No, he's not gay, Matthew. Or if he is, *I* don't know it, and I don't think he does, either. He's certainly given no evidence of it here, and God knows he wouldn't have had any trouble finding someone who would have been thrilled to take him home. He's absolutely gorgeous.'

'Not your type though, is he?'

'Not *my* type at all. I like dirty little boys myself. As you well know.'

'As I well know.'

'As everybody well knows, sweetheart.' Someone tapped a glass on the bar for service. 'Oh, keep it in your pants, Mary,' Kenny told him, in a mock British accent. 'I'm just having a spot of chat with a gent from the Yard.' To me he said, 'Speaking of Limey accents, he brought *her* here, you know. Or didn't you know? Well, you do now. Another drink? You already owe me for two doubles – the one you drank and the one you lost in the bet. Let's make it three.' He poured a generous double, set the bottle down. 'So naturally I guessed why you were here. This is not, after all, your normal watering hole. And they had been here both separately and together, and now she's dead and he's in the hotel with the bars on the windows, and the conclusion seemed inescapable. M. S. wants to know about J. B. and P. C.'

'The last part is certainly true.'

'Then ask questions of me.'

'He came here first by himself?'

'For the longest time he came here *only* by himself. I'd say he first showed up perhaps a year and a half ago. I would see him a couple of times a month, and always alone. Of course I didn't know anything about him at the time. He looked like law, but at the same time he didn't. Do you know what I mean? Maybe it was his clothes. No offense, but he dressed terribly well.'

'Why should I be offended?' He shrugged and moved off to tend to business. While he was gone I tried to figure out why Broadfield would patronize Sinthia's. The only way it made much sense was that there had been times when he wanted to get out of his apartment but didn't want to run into anybody he knew. A gay bar would have suited his needs perfectly.

When Kenny came back I said, 'You mentioned he showed up here with Portia Carr. When?'

'I can't be positive. He could have brought her here during the summer and I wouldn't have known about it. The first time I saw them together was – three weeks ago? It's hard for me to fix events temporally when I had no idea at the time that they would turn out to be important.'

'Was it before or after you knew who he was?'

'Ah, clever, clever! It was *after* I knew who he was, so three weeks is probably about right because I became familiar with his name when he first made contact with that investigator, and then I saw his photo in the newspaper, and then he turned up with the Amazon.'

'How many times were they here together?'

'At least twice. Maybe three times. That was all within the space of a week. May I replenish that drink for you?' I shook my head. 'Then I didn't see the two of them again, but I did see her.'

'Alone?'

'Briefly. She came in, sat at a table, ordered a drink.'

'When was this?'

'What's today, Friday? This would have been Tuesday night.'

'And she was killed Wednesday night.'

'Well, don't look at *me*, lover. *I* didn't do it.'

'I'll take your word for it.' I remembered the dimes I had dropped into various phones Tuesday night, calling Portia Carr's number and getting her answering machine. And she had been here then.

'Why did she come here, Kenny?'

'To meet someone.'

'Broadfield?'

'That's what I assumed, but the man who ultimately met her was a far cry indeed from Broadfield. It was hard to believe they were both members of the same species.'

'And he was the one she was waiting for?'

'Oh, absolutely. He walked in looking for her, and she had been looking up every time the door opened.'

He scratched his head for a moment. 'I don't know if she knew him or not. By sight, I mean. I have a vague feeling that she didn't, but I'm just guessing. This wasn't long ago, Matt, but I didn't really pay too much attention.'

'How long were they together?'

'They were together here for perhaps half an hour. Maybe a little longer than that. Then they left together, so they may have spent hours on end in one another's company. They didn't see fit to take me into their confidence.'

'And you don't know who the guy was.'

'Never saw him before or since.'

'What did he look like, Kenny?'

'Well, he didn't look like much, I'll tell you that. But you want a description rather than a critique, I would suppose. Let me just think.' He closed his eyes, drummed his fingers on the bartop. Without opening his eyes he said, 'A small person, Matt. Short, slender. Hollow cheeks. A great deal of forehead and an appalling absence of chin. Wore a rather tentative beard to conceal the lack of chin. No mustache. Heavy horn–rimmed glasses, so I didn't see his eyes and couldn't really swear that he had any, although I would guess that he did, as most people generally do. A left one and a right one, conventionally, although now and then – is something wrong?'

'Nothing's wrong, Ken.'

'Do you know him?'

'Yeah. I know him.'

I left Kenny's shortly after that. Then there's a stretch of time I don't remember clearly. I probably hit a bar or two. Eventually I found myself in the vestibule of Jerry Broadfield's building on Barrow Street.

I don't know what led me there or why I thought I ought to be there. But it must have made some sort of sense to me at the time.

A strip of celluloid popped the inner lock, and did the same job on the door to his apartment. Once inside his apartment, I locked the door and went around turning on lights, making myself at home. I found the bottle of bourbon and poured myself a drink, got a beer from the refrigerator for a chaser. I sat sipping bourbon and chasing it with beer. After a little while I turned on the radio and found a station that played unobtrusive music.

After some more bourbon and some more beer I took off my suit and hung it neatly in his closet. I got out of the rest of my clothes and found a pair of his pajamas in the bureau drawer. I put them on. I had to turn up the trouser bottoms because they were a little long on me. Aside from that they weren't a bad fit. A little loose, but not a bad fit.

Sometime just before I went to bed I picked up the telephone and dialed a number. I hadn't dialed it in a few days, but I still remembered it.

A deep voice with an English accent. 'Seven-two-five-five. I am sorry, but no one is at home at the moment. If you will leave your name and number at the sound of the tone, your call will be returned as soon as possible. Thank you.'

A gradual process, death. Someone had stabbed her

to death forty-eight hours ago in this very apartment, but her voice still answered her telephone.

I called two more times just to hear her voice. I didn't leave any messages. Then I had another can of beer and the rest of the bourbon and crawled into his bed and slept.

TWELVE

I woke up confused and disoriented, chasing the traces of a formless dream. For a moment I stood beside his bed in his pajamas and did not know where I was. Then memory flooded back, fully and completely. I took a quick shower, dried off, put my own clothes back on again. I had a can of beer for breakfast and got out of there, walking out into bright sunlight and feeling like a thief in the night.

I wanted to get moving right away. But I made myself have a big breakfast of eggs and bacon and toast and coffee at Jimmy Day's on Sheridan Square and drank a lot of coffee with it and then took the subway uptown.

There was a message waiting for me at my hotel, along with a lot of junk mail that went straight into the wastebasket. The message was from Seldon Wolk, who wanted me to call him at my convenience. I decided it was as convenient as it would ever be, and I called him from the hotel lobby.

His secretary put me through right away. He said, 'I saw my client this morning, Mr Scudder. He wrote out something for me to read to you. May I?'

'Go ahead.'

' "Matt – Don't know anything about Manch in connection with Portia. Is he a mayoral assistant? She had a few politicians in her book but wouldn't tell me who. I am not holding out on you anymore. I held out about Fuhrmann and our plans because I didn't see how it mattered and I like to keep things to myself. Forget all that. Thing to concentrate on is two cops who arrested me. How did they know to come to my apartment? Who tipped them? Work that angle." '

'That's all?'

'That's it, Mr Scudder. I feel like a messenger service, relaying questions and answers without understanding them. They might as well be in code. I trust the message makes some sense to you?'

'Some. How did Broadfield seem to you? Is he in good spirits?'

'Oh, very much so. Quite confident he'll be acquitted. I think his optimism is justified.' And he had a lot to say about various legal maneuvers that would keep Broadfield out of jail, or get his conviction reversed on appeal. I didn't bother listening, and when he slowed down a little I thanked him and said good-bye.

I stopped at the Red Flame for coffee and thought about Broadfield's message. His suggestion was all wrong, and after thinking about it for a while I realized why.

He was thinking like a cop. That was understandable – he had spent years learning to think like a cop, and it was hard to reorient yourself immediately. I still thought like a cop a lot of the time myself, and I'd had a few years to unlearn old habits. From a cop's point of view, it made very good sense to tackle the problem the way Broadfield wanted to. You stayed with hard data and you worked backward, tracking down every possible avenue of approach until you found out who had called in the homicide report. The odds were that the caller was also the murderer. If not, he'd probably seen something.

And if he hadn't, somebody else had. Someone may have seen Portia Carr enter the Barrow Street building on the night of her death. She hadn't entered it alone. Someone had seen her walk in arm in arm with the person who subsequently killed her.

And that was the kind of thing a cop could have run down. The police department had two things that made that sort of investigation work for them – the manpower and the authority. And you needed both to bring it off. One man working alone was not going to get anywhere. One man, with not even a junior G-man badge to convince people they ought to talk to him, would not even begin to accomplish anything that way.

Especially when the police would not even cooperate with him in the first place. Especially when they were opposed to any investigation that might get Broadfield out of the hot seat.

So my approach had to be a very different one, and one that no policeman could be expected to approve. I had to find out who had killed her, and then I had to find the facts that might back up what I'd already doped out.

But first I had to find somebody.

A small person, Kenny had said. Short, slender. Hollow cheeks. A great deal of forehead and an appalling absence of chin. A tentative beard. No mustache. Heavy horn-rimmed glasses …

★

I dropped by Armstrong's first to check. He wasn't there and hadn't been in yet that morning. I thought about having a drink but decided I could tackle Douglas Fuhrmann without one.

Except that I didn't get the chance. I went to his rooming house and rang the bell, and the same slatternly woman answered it. She may have been wearing the same robe and slippers. Once again she told me she was full up and suggested I try three doors down the street.

'Doug Fuhrmann,' I said.

Her eyes took the trouble to focus on my face. 'Fourth floor front,' she said. She frowned a little. 'You were here before. Looking for him.'

'That's right.'

'Yeah, I thought I seen you before.' She rubbed her forefinger across her nose, wiped it on her robe. 'I don't know if he's in or not. You want to knock on his door, go ahead.'

'All right.'

'Don't mess with his door, though. He's got this burglar alarm set up, makes all kinds of noise. I can't even go in there to clean for him. He does his own cleaning, imagine that.'

'He's probably been with you longer than most.'

'Listen, he's been here longer than me. I been working here what? A year? Two years?' If she didn't know, I couldn't help her out. 'He's been here years and years.'

'I guess you know him pretty well.'

'Don't know him at all. Don't know any of 'em. I

got no time to get to know people, mister. I got problems of my own, you can believe it.'

I believed it, but that didn't make me want to know what they were. She evidently wasn't going to be able to tell me anything about Fuhrmann, and I wasn't interested in whatever else she might tell me. I moved past her and climbed the stairs.

He wasn't in. I tried the knob, and the door was locked. It probably would have been easy enough to slip the bolt, but I didn't want to set the alarm off. I wonder if I would have remembered it if the old woman hadn't reminded me.

I wrote a note to the effect that it was important he get in touch with me immediately. I signed my name, added my telephone number, slipped the piece of paper under his door. Then I went downstairs and let myself out.

There was a Leon Manch listed in the Brooklyn book. The address was on Pierrepont Street, which would put him in Brooklyn Heights. I decided that was as good a place as any for a toilet slave to live. I dialed his number, and the phone rang a dozen times before I gave up.

I tried Prejanian's office. No one answered. Even crusaders only work a five-day week. I tried City Hall, wondering if Manch might have gone to the office. At least there was someone around there to answer the phone, even if there wasn't anyone present named Leon Manch.

The phone book had Abner Prejanian listed at 444 Central Park West. I had his number half-dialed when it struck me as pointless. He didn't know me from Adam and would hardly be inclined to cooperate with a total stranger over the telephone. I broke the connection, retrieved my dime, and looked up Claude Lorbeer. There was only one Lorbeer in Manhattan, a J. Lorbeer on West End Avenue. I tried the number, and when a woman answered I asked for Claude. When he came to the phone I asked him if he had had any contact with a man named Douglas Fuhrmann.

'I don't believe I've heard the name. In what context?'

'He's an associate of Broadfield's.'

'A policeman? I don't believe I've heard the name.'

'Maybe your boss did. I was going to call him, but he doesn't know me.'

'Oh, I'm glad you called me instead. I could call Mr Prejanian and ask him for you, and then I could get back to you. Anything else you'd want me to ask him?'

'Find out if the name Leon Manch rings any kind of a bell with him. In connection with Broadfield, that is.'

'Certainly. And I'll get right back to you, Mr Scudder.'

He rang back within five minutes. 'I just spoke to Mr Prejanian. Neither of the names you mentioned were familiar to him. Uh, Mr Scudder? I'd avoid any direct confrontation with Mr Prejanian if I were you.'

'Oh?'

'He wasn't precisely thrilled that I was cooperating with you. He didn't say so right out, but I think you understand what I'm getting at. He'd prefer that his staff pursue a policy of benign neglect, if I can revive that phrase. Of course you'll keep it between us that I said as much, won't you?'

'Of course.'

'You still remain convinced that Broadfield is innocent?'

'More now than ever.'

'And this man Fuhrmann holds the key?'

'He might. Things are starting to come together.'

'It sounds fascinating,' he said. 'Well, I won't keep you. If there's anything I can do, just give me a ring, but do let's keep it confidential, shall we?'

A little later I called Diana. We arranged to meet at eight-thirty at a French restaurant on Ninth Avenue, the Brittany du Soir. It is a quiet and private place where we would have a chance to be quiet and private people.

'I'll see you at eight-thirty then,' she said. 'Have you been making any headway? Oh, you can tell me when you see me.'

'Right.'

'I've done so much thinking, Matthew. I wonder if you know what it's like. I've spent so much time *not* thinking, almost willing myself not to think, and it's as though something has been unleashed. I shouldn't say all this. I'll just frighten you.'

'Don't worry about it.'

'That's what's strange. I'm not worried. Wouldn't you say that was strange?'

On my way back to the hotel I stopped at Fuhrmann's building. The manager didn't answer my ring. I guess she was busy with some of the problems she'd alluded to. I let myself in and climbed the stairs. He wasn't in and evidently hadn't been in — I could see the note I'd left him under his door.

I wished I'd taken down his phone number. Assuming he had a phone — I hadn't seen one on my visit, but his desk had been cluttered. He could have had a phone under one of those piles of paper.

I went home again, showered, shaved, straightened up the room. The maid had given it a cursory cleaning, and there wasn't much more I could do. It would always look like what it was, a small room in an unprepossessing hotel. Fuhrmann had chosen to transform his furnished room into an extension of himself. I had left mine as I found it. Initially I had found its stark simplicity somehow fitting. Now I had long since ceased to notice it, and only the prospect of entertaining a guest within it made me aware of its appearance.

I checked the liquor supply. There looked to be enough for me, and I didn't know what she preferred to drink. The store across the street would deliver until eleven.

Put on my best suit. Dabbed on a little cologne. The boys had given it to me for a Christmas present. I wasn't even sure which Christmas and couldn't remember when I'd used it last. Dabbed some on and felt ridiculous, but in a way that was not unpleasant.

Stopped at Armstrong's. Fuhrmann had been in and out an hour or so earlier. I left him a note. Called Manch, and this time he answered the phone.

I said, 'Mr Manch, my name is Matthew Scudder. I'm a friend of Portia Carr's.'

There was a pause, a long enough one to make his

reply unconvincing. 'I'm afraid I don't know anyone by that name.'

'I'm sure you do. You don't want to try that stance, Mr Manch. It's not going to work.'

'What do you want?'

'I want to see you. Sometime tomorrow.'

'What about?'

'I'll tell you when I see you.'

'I don't understand. What did you say your name was?'

I told him.

'Well, I don't understand, Mr Scudder. I don't know what you want from me.'

'I'll be at your place tomorrow afternoon.'

'I don't—'

'Tomorrow afternoon,' I said. 'Around three. It would be a very good idea for you to be there.'

He started to say something, but I didn't stay on the line long enough to hear it. It was a few minutes past eight. I went outside and walked down Ninth toward the restaurant.

THIRTEEN

We sat in a booth. She wore a simple black sheath and no jewelry. Her perfume was a floral scent with an undertone of spice. I ordered dry vermouth on the rocks for her and bourbon for myself. The conversation stayed light and airy through the first round of drinks. When we ordered a second round we also gave the waitress the dinner order – sweetbreads for her, a steak for me. The drinks came, and we touched glasses again, and our eyes met and led us into a silence that was just the slightest bit awkward.

She broke it. She extended her hand and I took it, and she lowered her eyes and said, 'I'm not terribly good at this. Out of practice, I guess.'

'So am I.'

'You've had a few years to get used to being a bachelor. I've had one little affair, and it wasn't really very much of anything. He was married.'

'You don't have to talk about it.'

'Oh, I know that. He was married, it was very casual and purely physical, and to be honest it wasn't even that wonderful physically. And it didn't last very long.' She hesitated. She may have been waiting for me to say something, but I remained silent. Then she said, 'You may want this to be, oh, casual, and that's all right, Matthew.'

'I don't think we can be casual with each other.'

'No, I don't suppose we can. I wish — I don't know what I wish.' She lifted her glass and sipped. 'I'm probably going to get a little bit drunk tonight. Is that a bad idea?'

'It might be a good idea. Shall we have wine with the meal?'

'I'd like that. I suppose it's a bad sign, having to get a little drunk.'

'Well, I'm the last person to tell you it's a bad idea. I get a little bit drunk every day of my life.'

'Is that something I should be worried about?'

'I don't know. It's damned well something you should be aware of, Diana. You ought to know who you're getting involved with.'

'Are you an alcoholic?'

'Well, what's an alcoholic? I suppose I drink enough alcohol to qualify. It doesn't keep me from functioning. Yet. I suppose it will eventually.'

'Could you stop drinking? Or cut down?'

'Probably. If I had a reason.'

The waitress brought our appetizers. I ordered a carafe of red wine. Diana impaled a mussel with a little fork, paused with it halfway to her mouth. 'Maybe we shouldn't talk about this yet.'

'Maybe not.'

'I think we feel the same about most things. I think what we want is the same, and I think our fears are the same.'

'Or pretty close, at least.'

'Yes. Maybe you're no bargain, Matthew. I think that's what you've been trying to tell me. I'm no bargain myself. I don't drink, but I might as well. I just

147

found a different way to retire from the human race. I gave up being me. I feel—'

'Yes?'

'As if I've got a second chance. As if I had that chance all along, but you only have it when you know you have it. And I don't know if you're a part of that chance or if you just made me aware of it.' She put her fork on her plate, the mussel still gripped by the tines. 'Oh, I'm enormously confused. All the magazines tell me I'm just the right age for an identity crisis. Is that what this is or am I falling in love and how do you tell the difference? Do you have a cigarette?'

'I'll get some. What brand do you smoke?'

'I don't smoke. Oh, any brand. Winstons, I guess.'

I got a pack from the machine. I opened it, gave her a cigarette, took one for myself. I struck a match and her fingers fastened around my wrist as she got her cigarette going. The tips of her fingers were very cool.

She said, 'I have three young children. I have a husband in jail.'

'And you're taking up drinking and smoking. You're a mess, all right.'

'And you're a sweet man. Have I told you that before? It's still true.'

I saw to it that she had most of the wine with dinner. Afterward she had a pot of espresso and a little snifter of brandy. I went back to coffee and bourbon. We did a lot of talking and shared a lot of long silences. These last were as communicative in their own way as our conversations.

It was close to midnight when I settled the tab. They

were anxious to close, but our waitress had been very decent about letting us alone. I showed my appreciation of her forbearance with a tip that was probably excessive. I didn't care. I loved the whole world.

We went out and stood on Ninth Avenue drinking the cold air. She discovered the moon and shared it with me. 'It's almost full. Isn't it beautiful?'

'Yes.'

'Sometimes I think I can almost feel the pull of the moon. Silly, isn't it?'

'I don't know. The sea feels it. That's why there are tides. And there's no denying that the moon influences human behavior. All cops know that. The crime rate changes with the moon.'

'Honest?'

'Uh-huh. Especially the weird crimes. The full moon makes people do odd things.'

'Like what?'

'Like kissing in public.'

A little later she said, 'Well, I don't know that that's odd. I think it's nice, actually.'

At Armstrong's I ordered coffee and bourbon for both of us. 'Because I like the feeling I'm getting Matthew, but I don't want to get sleepy. And I liked the way it tasted the other day.'

When she brought the drinks, Trina handed me a slip of paper. 'He was in about an hour ago,' she said. 'Before then he called a couple of times. He's very anxious for you to get in touch with him.'

'I unfolded the slip of paper. Doug Fuhrmann's name and a telephone number.

I said, 'Thanks. It's nothing that can't wait until morning.'

'He said it was urgent.'

'Well, that's one man's opinion.' Diana and I poured our bourbon into our coffee, and she asked me what it was about. 'A guy who's been close to your husband,' I said. 'He was also getting close to the girl who was murdered. I think I know why, but I want to talk to him about it.'

'Do you want to call him? Or see him for a while? Don't pass him up on my account, Matthew.'

'He can wait.'

'If you think it's important—'

'It's not. He can wait until tomorrow.'

Evidently Fuhrmann didn't think so. A little later the phone rang. Trina answered it and made her way to our table. 'Same caller,' she said. 'Do you want to talk to him?'

I shook my head. 'I was in,' I said. 'I got his message and said something about calling him in the morning. And then I had a drink and left.'

'Gotcha.'

Ten or twenty minutes later we did leave. Esteban was swinging the midnight-to-eight shift at the desk of my hotel. He gave me three messages, all of them from Fuhrmann.

'No calls,' I told him. 'No matter who. I'm not in.'

'Right.'

'If the phone rings I'll figure the building's on fire because otherwise I don't want any calls.'

'I understand.'

We rode up in the elevator, walked down the

hallway to my door. I opened it and stood aside to let her in. With her at my side the little room looked starker and more barren than ever.

'I thought of other places we could go,' I told her. 'A better hotel or a friend's apartment, but I decided that I wanted you to see where I live.'

'I'm glad, Matthew.'

'Is it all right?'

'Of course it's all right.'

We kissed. We held each other for a long time. I smelled her perfume and tasted the sweetness of her mouth. After a time I released her. She moved slowly and deliberately around my room, examining things, getting a sense of the place. Then she turned to me and smiled a very gentle smile, and we began undressing.

FOURTEEN

All through the night one of us would wake and awaken the other. Then I woke up for the last time and found I was alone. Pale sunlight filtered by bad air gave the room a golden cast. I got out of bed and picked my watch up from the bedside table. It was almost noon.

I had almost finished dressing when I found her note. It was wedged between the glass and the frame of the mirror over my dresser. Her handwriting was very neat and quite small.

I read:

Darling –
  What is it that the children say? Last night was the first night of the rest of my life. I have so much to say, but I am in no condition to express my thoughts well.
  Please call me. And call me, please,

                                                              Your Lady

I read it through a couple of times. Then I folded it carefully and tucked it into my wallet.

There was a single message in my box. Fuhrmann had called a final time around one-thirty. Then he had evidently given up and gone to sleep. I called him from the lobby and got a busy signal. I went out and had some breakfast. The air, which had looked to be polluted from my window, tasted clean enough on the street. Maybe it was my mood. I hadn't felt this well in a long time.

I got up from the table again and called Fuhrmann again after my second cup of coffee. The line was still busy. I went back and had a third cup and smoked one of the cigarettes I had bought for Diana. She had had three or four the previous night, and I had smoked one each time she did. I burned up about half of this one, left the pack on the table, tried Fuhrmann a third time, paid my check, and walked over to Armstrong's just to check if he was there or had been in yet. He wasn't and hadn't.

Something hovered on the edge of consciousness, whining plaintively at me. I used the pay phone at Armstrong's to call him again. The same busy signal, and it sounded different to me from the usual sort of busy signal. I called the operator and told her I wanted to know if a certain number was engaged or if the telephone was simply off the hook. I got a girl who evidently didn't speak much English and wasn't sure how to perform the task I'd asked of her. She offered to put me in touch with her supervisor, but I was only half a dozen blocks from Fuhrmann's place, so I told her not to bother.

I was quite calm when I set out for his place and extremely anxious by the time I got there. Maybe I was picking up signals and they were coming in stronger as the distance decreased. But for one reason or another I didn't ring the bell in his vestibule. I looked inside and saw no one around, and then I used my piece of celluloid to slip the lock.

I climbed the stairs to the top floor without running

into anyone. The building was absolutely silent. I went to Fuhrmann's door and knocked on it, called his name, knocked again.

Nothing.

I took out my strip of celluloid and looked at it and at the door. I thought about the burglar alarm. If it was going to go off I wanted to have the door open by the time it began to make noises so I could get the hell out of there. Which ruled out slipping the bolt back. Subtlety has its uses, but sometimes brute force is called for.

I kicked the door in. It only took one kick because the dead bolt had not been set. You need the key to set the dead bolt, just as you need a key to set the alarm, and the person who had last left Fuhrmann's apartment had not had those keys or had not troubled to use them. So the alarm did not go off, which was all to the good, but that was all the good news I was going to get.

The bad news was waiting for me inside, but I'd known what it would be from the instant the alarm had failed to sound. In a sense I'd known before I even reached the building but that was instinctive knowledge, and when the alarm stayed quiet it became deductive knowledge, and now that I could see him it was just cold, hard fact.

He was dead. He was lying on the floor in front of his desk, and it looked as though he had been leaning over his desk when his killer took him. I didn't have to touch him to know he was dead. The left rear portion of his skull was pulped, and the room itself reeked of death. Dead colons and bladders divest themselves of their contents. Corpses, before the working of the

154

undertaker's art, smell as foul as the death that grips them.

I touched him anyway to guess how long he'd been dead. But his flesh was cold, so I could only know that he'd been dead a minimum of five or six hours. I'd never bothered to pick up much knowledge of forensic medicine. The lab boys handle that area, and they're reasonably good at it, if not half so good as they like to pretend.

I went over to the door and closed it. The lock was useless, but there was a plate for a police lock on the floor, and I found the steel bar and set it in place. I didn't intend to stay long but wanted no interruptions while I was there.

The phone was off the hook. There were no other signs of a struggle, so I assumed the killer had taken the phone off the hook to retard discovery of the body. If he was that cute, there weren't going to be any prints around, but I still took the trouble not to add any of my own or smear any that he might inadvertently have made.

When had he been killed? The bed was unmade, but perhaps he didn't make it every day. Men who live alone often don't. Had it been made up when I'd visited him? I thought about it and decided I couldn't be certain one way or the other. I recalled an impression of neatness and precision, which suggested it had indeed been made up, but there was also an impression of comfort, which would mesh well enough with an unmade bed. The more I thought about it, the more I decided it didn't make any difference one way or the other. The medical examiner would fix the time of death, and I was in no rush to know what I would learn from him soon enough.

So I sat on the edge of the bed and looked at Doug Fuhrmann and tried to remember the precise sound of his voice and the way his face had looked.

He had tried to reach me. Over and over again, and I wouldn't take his calls. Because I was a little peeved with him for holding out on me. Because I was with a woman who was using up all my attention, and that was such a novel experience for me that I hadn't wanted it diluted even for a moment.

And if I'd taken his call? Well, he might have told me something that he would never tell me now. But it was more likely that he would only confirm what I had already guessed about his relationship with Portia Carr.

If I'd taken his call, would he be alive now?

I could have wasted the whole day sitting on his bed and asking myself that sort of question. And whatever its answer, I had already wasted enough time.

I unlocked the police lock, opened the door a crack. The hallway was empty. I let myself out of Fuhrmann's room and went down the stairs and out of the building without encountering anyone at all.

Midtown North — it used to be the Eighteenth Precinct — is on West Fifty-fourth just a few blocks from where I was. I rang them from a booth in a saloon called the Second Chance. There were two wine drinkers at the bar and what looked to be a third wino behind it. When the phone was answered I gave Fuhrmann's address and said that a man had been murdered there. I replaced the receiver while the duty officer was patiently asking me my name.

★

I was in too much of a hurry to take a cab. The subway was faster. I rode it to the Clark Street station just over the bridge in Brooklyn. I had to ask directions to get to Pierrepont Street.

The block was mostly brownstones. The building where Leon Manch lived was fourteen stories tall, a giant among its fellows. The doorman was a stocky black with three deep horizontal lines running across his forehead.

'Leon Manch,' I said.

He shook his head. I reached for my notebook, checked his address, looked up at the doorman.

'You have the right address,' he said. His accent was West Indian, and the *a*'s came out very broad. 'You come the wrong day is all the problem.'

'I'm expected.'

'Mr Manch, he is not here no more.'

'He moved out?' It seemed impossible.

'He doan' want to wait for the elevator,' he said. 'So he take a shortcut.'

'What are you talking about?'

The jive, I decided later, was not flippancy; it was an attempt to speak around the edges of the unspeakable. Now, abandoning that tack, he said, 'He jump out the window. Land right there.' He pointed to a portion of the sidewalk that looked no different from the rest. 'He land there,' he repeated.

'When?'

'Las' night.' He touched his forehead, then made a sign similar to genuflection. I don't know whether it was a personal ritual or part of a religion with which I was unfamiliar. 'Armand was working then. If I am working and man jump out window, I doan' know what I do.'

'Was he killed?'

He looked at me. 'What you think, man? Mr Manch, he lives on fourteen. What you think?'

The nearest precinct house, and the one that figured to have the case, was on Joralemon near Borough Hall. I got lucky there – I recognized a cop named Kinsella whom I'd worked with some years back. And I was lucky a second time because he evidently hadn't heard I'd gone to work for Jerry Broadfield, so he had no reason not to cooperate with me.

'Happened last night,' he said. 'I wasn't on when it happened, but it looks to be pretty clear cut, Matt.' He shuffled some papers, set them down on the desk. 'Manch lived alone. I suppose he was a fruit. A guy living alone in that neighborhood, you can draw your own conclusions. Nine out of ten he's gay.'

And one out of ten he's a toilet slave.

'Let's see now. Went out the window, did a header, dead on arrival at Adelphi Hospital. Identification based on contents of pockets and clothing labels plus which window was open.'

'No identification by next of kin?'

'Not that I know of. Nothing listed here. Any question that it's him? If you want to go take a look at him it's your business, but he landed headfirst, so—'

'I never saw him, anyway. He was alone when he went out the window?' Kinsella nodded. 'Any eyewitnesses?'

'No. But he left a note. It was in a typewriter on his desk.'

'Was the note typewritten?'

'It doesn't say.'

'I don't suppose I could have a look at the note?'

'Not a chance, Matt. I don't have access to it myself. You want to talk to the officer in charge, that's Lew Marko, he'll be coming on duty sometime tonight. Maybe he can help you out.'

'I don't suppose it matters.'

'Wait a minute, the wording's copied down here. This help you at all?'

I read:

Forgive me. I cannot go on this way. I have lived a bad life.

Nothing about murder.

Could he have done it? A lot depended on when Fuhrmann was killed, and I wouldn't know that until I found out what the medical examiner learned. Say Manch killed Fuhrmann, came home, was overtaken by remorse, opened his window –

I didn't like it much.

I said, 'What time did he do it, Jim? I don't see it listed.'

He looked through the records, frowning. 'There ought to be a time here. I don't see it. He was DOA at Adelphi at eleven thirty-five last night, but that don't tell us what time he went out the window.'

But then again it didn't really have to. Doug Fuhrmann made his final call to me at one-thirty, an hour and fifty-five minutes after a physician pronounced Leon Manch dead.

I liked it better that way the more I thought about it. Because everything was starting to fall into place for me, and the way it was breaking Manch wasn't Fuhrmann's killer or Portia Carr's killer, either. Maybe Manch was Manch's killer, maybe he'd typed a suicide note because he couldn't find a pen, maybe his remorse was compounded of disgust with the life of a toilet slave. *I have lived a bad life* – well, who the hell has not?

For the time being, it didn't matter whether Manch had killed himself or not. Maybe he'd had help, but that was something I couldn't know yet and didn't have to know how to prove.

I knew who had killed the other two, Portia and Doug. I knew it in much the same way that I had known before reaching his building that Doug Fuhrmann would be dead. We call such knowledge the product of intuition because we cannot precisely chart the working of the mind. It goes on playing computer while our consciousness is directed elsewhere.

I knew the killer's name. I had some strong ideas about his motive. I had more ground to cover before it would all be wrapped up, but the hard part was over. Once you know what you're looking for, the rest comes easy.

FIFTEEN

It was another three or four hours before I got out of a cab in the West Seventies and gave my name to a doorman. It was not the first taxi I'd taken since I got back from Brooklyn. I had had to see several people. I'd been offered drinks but hadn't accepted any. I had had some coffee, including a couple of cups of the best coffee I'd ever had.

The doorman announced me, then steered me to the elevator. I rode upstairs to the sixth floor, found the appropriate door, knocked. The door was opened by a small, birdlike woman with blue-gray hair. I introduced myself and she gave me her hand. 'My son's watching the football game,' she said. 'Do you care for football? I don't find it of any real interest myself. Now you just have a seat and I'll tell Claude you're here.'

But it wasn't necessary to tell him. He was standing in an archway at the rear of the living room. He wore a sleeveless brown cardigan over a white shirt. He had bedroom slippers on his feet. The thumbs of his pudgy hands were hooked into his belt. He said, 'Good afternoon, Mr Scudder. Won't you come this way? Mom, Mr Scudder and I will be in the den.'

I followed him into a small room in which several overstuffed chairs were grouped around a color television set. On the large screen an oriental girl was bowing before a bottle of men's cologne.

'Cable,' Lorbeer said. 'Makes for absolutely perfect reception. And it only costs a couple of dollars a month. Before we signed up for it we just never got really satisfactory reception.'

'You've lived here a long time?'

'All my life. Well, not quite. We moved here when I was about two-and-a-half years old. Of course my father was alive then. This was his room, his study.'

I looked around. There were English hunting prints on the walls, several racks of pipes, a few framed photographs. I walked over to the door and closed it. Lorbeer noted this without commenting.

I said, 'I spoke to your employer.'

'Mr Prejanian?'

'Yes. He was very pleased to hear that Jerry Broadfield will be released soon. He said he's not sure how much use he'll get out of Broadfield's testimony but that he's glad to see the man won't be convicted of a crime he didn't commit.'

'Mr Prejanian's a very generous man.'

'Is he?' I shrugged. 'I didn't get that impression myself, but I'm sure you know him better than I do. What I sensed was that he's glad to see Broadfield proved innocent because his own organization doesn't look so bad now. So he was hoping all along that Broadfield would turn out to be innocent.' I watched him carefully. 'He says he'd have been glad to know earlier that I was working for Broadfield.'

'Really.'

'Uh-huh. That's what he said.'

Lorbeer moved closer to the television set. He rested a hand on top of it and looked down at the back of his hand. 'I've been having hot chocolate,' he said. 'Sundays are days of complete regression for me. I sit around in comfy old clothes and watch sports on television and sip hot chocolate. I don't suppose you'd care for a cup?'

'No, thank you.'

'A drink? Something stronger?'

'No.'

He turned to look at me. The pairs of parenthetical lines on either side of his little mouth seemed to be more deeply etched now. 'Of course I can't be expected to bother Mr Prejanian with every little thing that comes up. That's one of my functions, screening him from trivia. His time is very valuable, and there are already far too many demands on it.'

'That's why you didn't bother to call him yesterday. You told me you'd spoken with him, but you hadn't. And you warned me to route inquiries through you so as to avoid antagonizing Prejanian.'

'Just doing my job, Mr Scudder. It's possible I committed a judgmental error. No one is perfect, nor have I ever claimed perfection.'

I leaned over, turned off the television set. 'It's a distraction,' I explained. 'We should both pay attention to this. You're a murderer, Claude, and I'm afraid you're not going to get away with it. Why don't you sit down?'

'That's a ridiculous accusation.'

'Have a seat.'

'I'm quite comfortable standing. You've just made a completely absurd charge. I don't understand it.'

I said, 'I suppose I should have thought about you

right at the beginning. But there was a problem. Whoever killed Portia Carr had to connect up with Broadfield in one way or another. She was killed in his apartment, so she had to be killed by someone who knew where his apartment was, somebody who took the trouble to decoy him out of it first and send him off to Bay Ridge on a wild-goose chase.'

'You're assuming Broadfield is innocent. I still don't see any reason to be sure of that.'

'Oh, I knew he was innocent for a dozen reasons.'

'Even so, didn't the Carr woman know about Broadfield's apartment?'

I nodded. 'As a matter of fact, she did. But she couldn't have led her killer there because she was unconscious when she made the trip. She was hit on the head first and then stabbed. It stood to reason that she'd been hit elsewhere. Otherwise the killer would have just gone on hitting her until she was dead. He wouldn't have stopped to pick up a knife. But what you did, Claude, was knock her out somewhere else and then get her to Broadfield's apartment. By then you'd disposed of whatever you'd hit her with, so you finished the job with a knife.'

'I think I'll have a cup of chocolate. You're sure you wouldn't care for some?'

'Positive. I didn't want to believe a cop would kill Portia Carr in order to frame Broadfield. Everything pointed that way, but I didn't like the feel of it. I preferred the idea that framing Broadfield was a handy way to get away with murder, that the killer's main object was to get rid of Portia. But then how would he know about Broadfield's apartment and phone number? What I needed was somebody who was connected to both of them. And I found somebody, but there was no motive apparent.'

'You must mean me,' he said calmly. 'Since I certainly had no motive. But then I didn't know the Carr person either, and barely knew Broadfield, so your reasoning breaks down, doesn't it?'

'Not you. Douglas Fuhrmann. He was going to ghostwrite Broadfield's book. That's why Broadfield had turned informer – he wanted to be somebody important and write a best-seller. He got the idea from Carr because she was going to go the Happy Hooker one better. Fuhrmann got the idea of playing both ends and got in touch with Carr to see if he could write her book, too. That's what tied the two of them together – it has to be – but it's not a murder motive.'

'Then why am I elected? Because you don't know of anyone else?'

I shook my head. 'I knew it was you before I really knew why. I asked you yesterday afternoon if you knew anything about Doug Fuhrmann. You knew enough about him to go over to his house last night and kill him.'

'This is remarkable. Now I'm being accused of the murder of a man I never heard of.'

'It won't work, Claude. Fuhrmann was a threat to you because he'd been talking with both of them, with Carr and with Broadfield. He was trying to reach me last night. If I'd had time to see him, maybe you wouldn't have been able to kill him. And maybe you would have, because maybe he didn't know what he knew. You were one of Portia Carr's clients.'

'That's a filthy lie.'

'Maybe it's filthy. I wouldn't know. I don't know what you did with her or what she did with you. I could make some educated guesses.'

'Damn you, you're an animal.' He didn't raise his voice, but the loathing in it was fierce. 'I will thank you not to talk like that in the same house with my mother.'

I just looked at him. He met my eyes with confidence at first, and then his face seemed to melt. All the resolve went out of it. His shoulders sagged, and he looked at once much older and much younger. Just a middle-aged little boy.

'Knox Hardesty knew,' I went on. 'So you killed Portia for nothing. I can pretty much figure out what happened, Claude. When Broadfield turned up at Prejanian's office, you learned about more than police corruption. You learned through Broadfield that Portia was in Knox Hardesty's pocket, feeding him her client list in order to escape deportation. You were on that list and you figured it was just a question of time before she handed you over to him.

'So you got Portia to press charges against Broadfield, accusing him of extortion. You wanted to give him a motive for killing her, and that was an easy one to arrange. She thought you were a cop when you called her, and it was easy enough for her to go along with it. One way or another, you managed to scare her pretty well. Whores are easy to scare.

'At this point you had Broadfield set up beautifully. You didn't even have to be particularly brilliant about

166

the murder itself because the cops would be so anxious to tie it to Broadfield. You decoyed Portia to the Village at the same time that you sent Broadfield off to Brooklyn. Then you knocked her out, dragged her into his apartment, killed her, and got out of there. You dropped the knife in a sewer, washed your hands, and came on home to Mama.'

'Leave my mother out of this.'

'That bothers you, doesn't it? My mentioning your mother?'

'Yes, it does.' He was squeezing his hands together as if to control them. 'It bothers me a great deal. That's why you're doing it, I suppose.'

'Not entirely, Claude.' I drew a breath. 'You shouldn't have killed her. There was no point to it. Hardesty already knew about you. If he'd thrown your name into the open at the beginning, a lot of time would have been saved and Fuhrmann and Manch would still be alive. But—'

'Manch?'

'Leon Manch. It looked as though he might have killed Fuhrmann, but the timing was wrong. And then it looked as though you might have set it up, but you would have done it better. You would have killed them in the right order, wouldn't you? First Fuhrmann and then Manch, and not the other way around.'

'I don't know what you're talking about.'

And this time he evidently didn't, and the difference in his tone was obvious. 'Leon Manch was another name on Portia's client list. He was also Knox Hardesty's pipeline into the mayor's office. I called him yesterday afternoon and arranged to see him, and I guess he couldn't handle it. He jumped out a window last night.'

'He actually killed himself.'

'It looks that way.'

'He could have killed Portia Carr.' He said it not argumentatively but thoughtfully.

I nodded. 'He could have killed her, yes. But he couldn't have killed Fuhrmann because Fuhrmann made a couple of telephone calls after Manch had been officially pronounced dead. You see what that means, Claude?'

'What?'

'All you had to do was leave that little writer alone. You couldn't know it, but that was all you had to do. Manch left a note. He didn't confess to murder, but it could have been interpreted that way. I would certainly have interpreted it that way and I would have done everything possible to pin the Carr murder on Manch's dead body. If I managed it, Broadfield was clear. If not, he would stand trial himself. Either way, you would have been home free because I would have settled on Manch as the killer and the cops had already settled on Broadfield and that left nobody in the world hunting for you.'

He said nothing for a long time. Then he narrowed his eyes and said, 'You're trying to trap me.'

'You're already trapped.'

'She was an evil, filthy woman.'

'And you were the Lord's avenging angel.'

'No. Nothing of the sort. You are trying to trap me, and it won't work. You can't prove a thing.'

'I don't have to.'

'Oh?'

'I want you to come over to the police station with me, Claude. I want you to confess to the murders of Portia Carr and Douglas Fuhrmann.'

'You must be insane.'

'No.'

'Then you must think I'm insane. Why on earth would I do something like that? Even if I did commit murder—'

'To spare yourself, Claude.'

'I don't understand.'

I looked at my watch. It was still early, and I felt as though I'd been awake for months.

'You said I can't prove anything,' I told him. 'And I said you were right. But the police can prove it. Not now, but after they've spent some time digging. Knox Hardesty can establish that you were a client of Portia Carr's. He gave me the information once I was able to show him how it was bound up in murder, and he'll hardly hold it back in court. And you can bet that somebody saw you with Portia in the Village and somebody saw you on Ninth Avenue when you killed Fuhrmann. There's always a witness, and when the police and the district attorney's office are both putting in time, the witnesses tend to turn up.'

'Then let them turn up these people if they exist. Why should I confess to make things easier for them?'

'Because you'd be making things easier for yourself, Claude. So much easier.'

'That doesn't make sense.'

'If the police dig, they'll get everything, Claude. They'll find out why you were seeing Portia Carr.

Right now nobody knows. Hardesty doesn't know, I don't know, no one does. But if they dig, they'll find out. And there will be insinuations in the newspapers, and people will suspect things, perhaps they'll suspect worse than the truth—'

'Stop it.'

'Everyone will know about it, Claude.' I inclined my head toward the closed door. 'Everyone,' I said.

'Damn you.'

'You could spare her that knowledge, Claude. Of course a confession might also get you a lighter sentence. It theoretically can't happen in Murder One, but you know how the game is played. It certainly wouldn't hurt your chances. But I think that's a secondary consideration as far as you're concerned, Claude. Isn't it? I think you'd like to save yourself some scandal. Am I right?'

He opened his mouth but closed it without speaking.

'You could keep your motive a secret, Claude. You could invent something. Or just refuse to explain. No one would pressure you, not if you'd already confessed to homicide. People close to you would know you had committed murder, but they wouldn't have to know other things about your life.'

He lifted his cup of chocolate to his lips. He sipped it, returned it to its saucer.

'Claude—'

'Just let me think for a moment, will you?'

'All right.'

I don't know how long we remained like that, me standing, him seated before the silent television set. Say five minutes. Then he sighed, scuffed off his slippers, reached to put on a pair of shoes. He tied them and got to his feet. I walked to the door and opened it and stood aside so he could precede me through it into the living room.

He said, 'Mother, I'll be going out for a little while. Mr Scudder needs my help. Something important has come up.'

'Oh, but your dinner, Claude. It's almost ready. Perhaps your friend would care to join us?'

I said, 'I'm afraid not, Mrs Lorbeer.'

'There's just no time, Mother,' Claude agreed. 'I'll have to have dinner out.'

'Well, if it can't be helped.'

He squared his shoulders, went to the front closet for a coat. 'Now wear your heavy overcoat,' she told him. 'It's turned quite cold outside. It is cold out, isn't it, Mr Scudder?'

'Yes,' I said. 'It's very cold out.'

SIXTEEN

My second trip to the Tombs was very different from my first. It was about the same hour of the day, around eleven in the morning, but this time I'd had a good, full night's sleep and very little to drink the night before. I'd seen him in a cell the first time. Now I was meeting him and his lawyer at the front desk. He had left all that tension and depression in his cell and he looked like the conquering hero.

He and Seldon Wolk were already on hand when I walked in. Broadfield's face lit up at the sight of me. 'There's my man,' he called out. 'Matt, baby, you're the greatest. Absolutely the greatest. If I did one intelligent thing in my life, it was getting hooked up with you.' And he was pumping my hand and beaming down at me. 'Didn't I tell you I was getting out of this toilet? And didn't you turn out to be the guy to spring me?' He inclined his head conspiratorially, lowered his voice to a near-whisper. 'And I'm a guy knows how to say thank you so you know I mean it. You got a bonus coming, buddy.'

'You paid me enough.'

'The hell I did. What's a man's life worth?'

I had asked myself the same question often enough, but not in quite the same way. I said, 'I made something like five hundred dollars a day. That'll do me, Broadfield.'

'Jerry.'

'Sure.'

'And I say you got a bonus coming. You met my lawyer? Seldon Wolk?'

'We've spoken,' I said. Wolk and I shook hands and made polite sounds at each other.

'Well, it's about that time,' Broadfield said. 'I guess any reporters who're gonna show up are already waiting out there, don't you think? If any of 'em miss out, it'll teach 'em to be on time next shot. Is Diana out there with the car?'

'She's waiting where you wanted her to wait,' the lawyer told him.

'Perfect. You met my wife, didn't you, Matt? Of course you did, I gave you that note to take out there. What we gotta do, you get a woman, and the four of us'll have dinner one of these nights. We ought to get to know each other better, all of us.'

'We'll have to do that,' I agreed.

'Well,' he said. He tore open a manila envelope and shook out its contents on the top of the desk. He put his wallet into his pocket, slipped his watch onto his wrist, scooped up and pocketed a handful of coins. Then he put his tie around his neck and under his shirt collar and made an elaborate performance of tying it. 'Did I tell you, Matt? Thought I might have to tie it twice. But I think the knot looks just about right, don't you?'

'It looks fine.'

He nodded. 'Yeah,' he said. 'I think it looks pretty good, all right. I'll tell you something. Matt, I *feel* good. How do I look, Seldon?'

'You look fine.'

'I feel like a million dollars,' he said.

He handled the reporters pretty nicely. He answered
questions, striking a nice balance between sincere and
cocky, and while they still had questions to ask him he
flashed the number-one grin, gave a victorious wave,
and pushed through them and got into his car. Diana
stepped on the gas, and they drove down to the end of
the block and turned the corner. I stood there watching
until they were out of sight.

Of course she'd had to come to pick him up. And
she would take it easy for a day or two, and then she'd
let him know how things stood. She'd said she didn't
expect much trouble from him. She was certain he
didn't love her and that she had long since ceased to be
important in his life. But I was to give her a couple of
days, and then she would call.

'Well, that was pretty exciting,' a voice behind me
said. 'I figured maybe we were supposed to throw rice
at the happy couple, something like that.'

Without turning I said, 'Hello, Eddie.'

'Hello, Matt. Beautiful morning, isn't it?'

'Not bad.'

'I suppose you're feeling pretty good.'

'Not too bad.'

'Cigar?' Lieutenant Eddie Koehler didn't wait for an
answer, put the cigar in his own mouth and lit it. It
took him three matches because the wind blew out the
first two. 'I oughta get a lighter,' he said. 'You check
out that lighter Broadfield was using before? Looked
expensive.'

'I think it probably is.'

'Looked like gold to me.'

'Probably. Though gold and gold plate look pretty much the same.'

'They don't cost the same, though. Do they?'

'Not as a general rule.'

He smiled, swung out a hand, and gripped my upper arm. 'Aw, you son of a bitch,' he said. 'Lemme buy you a drink, you old son of a bitch.'

'It's a little early for me, Eddie. Maybe a cup of coffee.'

'Even better. Since when is it ever too early to buy you a drink?'

'Oh, I don't know. Maybe I'll take it a little easier on the booze, see if it makes a difference.'

'Yeah?'

'Well, for a while, anyway.'

He eyed me appraisingly. 'You sound like your old self a little, you know that? I can't remember the last time you sounded like this.'

'Don't make too much out of it, Eddie. All I'm doing is passing up a drink.'

'No, there's something else. I can't put my finger on it, but something's different.'

We went over to a little place on Reade Street and ordered coffee and Danish. He said, 'Well, you sprung the bastard. I hate to see him off the hook, but I can't hardly hold it against you. You got him off.'

'He shouldn't have been on in the first place.'

'Yeah, well, that's something else, isn't it?'

'Uh-huh. You ought to be glad the way things worked out. He's not going to be a tremendous amount of use to Abner Prejanian because Prejanian's going to have to keep a low profile for the next little while. He doesn't look too good himself now. His assistant just got nailed for killing two people and framing Abner's star witness. You were complaining that he loved to see his name in the papers. I think he's going to try to keep his name out of the papers for a couple of months, don't you?'

'Could be.'

'And Knox Hardesty doesn't look too good, either. He's all right as far as the public is concerned, but the word's going to get around that he's not very good at protecting his witnesses. He had Carr, and Carr gave him Manch, and they're both dead, and that's not a good track record to have when you're trying to get people to cooperate with you.'

'Of course he hasn't been bothering the department, anyway, Matt.'

'Not yet. But with Prejanian quiet he might have wanted to come on in. You know how it goes, Eddie. Whenever they want headlines they take a shot at the cops.'

'Yeah, that's the fucking truth.'

'So I didn't do so badly by you, did I? The department doesn't wind up looking bad.'

'No, you did all right, Matt.'

'Yeah.'

He picked up his cigar, puffed on it. It had gone out. He lit it again with a match and watched the match burn almost to his fingertips before shaking it out and dropping it into the ashtray. I chewed a bite of Danish and chased it with a gulp of coffee.

I could cut down on the drinking. There would be times when it got difficult. When I thought about Fuhrmann and how I could have taken that call from him. Or when I thought about Manch and his plunge to the ground. My phone call couldn't have done it all by itself. Hardesty had been pressuring him all along, and he'd been carrying a load of guilt for years. But I hadn't helped him, and maybe if I hadn't called –

Except you can't let yourself think that way. What you have to do is remind yourself that you caught one murderer and kept one innocent man out of prison. You never win them all, and you can't blame yourself whenever you drop one.

'Matt?' I looked at him. 'That conversation we had the other night. At that bar where you hang out?'

'Armstrong's.'

'Right, Armstrong's. I said some things I didn't have to say.'

'Oh, the hell with that, Eddie.'

'No hard feelings?'

'Of course not.'

Pause. 'Well, a few guys who knew I was gonna drop down today, which I was doing, figuring you'd be here, they asked me to let you know there's no hard feelings toward you. Not that there ever was in a general sense, just that they wished you weren't hooked up with Broadfield at the time, if you get my meaning.'

'I think I do.'

'And they hope you got no bad feelings toward the department, is all.'

'None.'

'Well, that's what I figured, but I thought I'd get it

out in the open and be sure.' He ran a hand over his forehead, ruffled his hair. 'You're really figuring to take it easier on the booze?'

'Might as well give it a try. Why?'

'I don't know. You think maybe you're ready to rejoin the human race?'

'I never resigned, did I?'

'You know what I'm talking about.'

I didn't say anything.

'You proved something, you know. You're still a good cop, Matt. It's what you're really good at.'

'So?'

'It's easier to be a good cop when you're carrying a badge.'

'Sometimes it's harder. If I'd had a badge this past week, I would have been told to lay off.'

'Yeah, and you were told that, anyway, and you didn't listen, and you wouldn't have listened, badge or no badge. Am I right?'

'Maybe. I don't know.'

'The best way to get a good police department is to keep good policemen in it. I'd like it a hell of a lot to see you back on the force.'

'I don't think so, Eddie.'

'I wasn't asking you to make a decision. I was saying you could think about it. And you can think it over for the next little while, can't you? Maybe it'll be something that starts to make sense when you don't have a skinful of booze in you twenty-four hours a day.'

'It's possible.'

'You'll think about it?'

'I'll think about it.'

'Uh-huh.' He stirred his coffee. 'You hear from your kids lately?'

'They're fine.'

'Well, that's good.'

'I'm taking them this Saturday. There's some kind of father–son thing with their Scout troop, a rubber-chicken dinner and then seats for the Nets game.'

'I could never get interested in the Nets.'

'They're supposed to have a good team.'

'Yeah, that's what they tell me. Well, it's great that you're seeing them.'

'Uh-huh.'

'Maybe you and Anita—'

'Drop it, Eddie.'

'Yeah, I talk too much.'

'She's got somebody else, anyway.'

'You can't expect her to sit around.'

'I don't, and I don't care. I've got somebody else myself.'

'Oh. For serious?'

'I don't know.'

'Something to take it slow and see what happens, I guess.'

'Something like that.'

That was Monday. For the next couple of days I took a lot of long walks and spent time at a lot of churches. I would have a couple of drinks in the evening to make it easier to get to sleep, but to all intents and purposes I wasn't doing any serious drinking at all. I walked around, I enjoyed the weather, I kept checking my telephone messages, I read the *Times* in the morning and the *Post* at night. I began wondering after a while why I wasn't getting the phone message I was waiting for, but I wasn't upset enough to pick up the phone and place a call myself.

Then Thursday around two in the afternoon I was walking along, not going anywhere in particular, and as I passed a newsstand at the corner of Fifty-seventh and Eighth, I happened to glance at the headline of the *Post*. I normally waited and bought the late edition, but the headline caught me and I bought the paper.

Jerry Broadfield was dead.

SEVENTEEN

When he sat down across from me, I knew who it was without raising my eyes. I said, 'Hi, Eddie.'

'Figured I'd find you here.'

'Not hard to guess, was it?' I waved a hand to signal Trina. 'What is it, Seagram's? Bring my friend here a Seagram's and water. I'll have another of these.' To him I said, 'It didn't take you long. I've only been here about an hour myself. Of course the news must have hit the street with the noon edition. I just didn't happen to see a paper until an hour ago. It says here that he got it around eight this morning. Is that right?'

'That's right, Matt. According to the report I saw.'

'He walked out the door and a late-model car pulled up at the curb and somebody gave him both barrels of a sawed-off shotgun. A school kid said the man with the gun was white but didn't know about the man in the car, the driver.'

'That's right.'

'One man's white and the car's described as blue and the gun was left at the scene. No prints, I don't suppose.'

'Probably not.'

'No way to trace the sawed-off, I don't guess.'

'I haven't heard, but—'

'But there won't be any way to trace it.'

'Doesn't figure to be.'

Trina brought the drinks. I picked mine up and said, 'Absent friends, Eddie.'

'Sure thing.'

'He wasn't your friend, and though you may not believe it, he was less my friend than yours, but that's how we'll drink the toast, to absent friends. I drank your toast the way you wanted it, so you can drink mine.'

'Whatever you say.'

'Absent friends,' I said.

We drank. The booze seemed to have more of a punch after a few days of taking it easy. I certainly hadn't lost my taste for it, though. It went down nice and easy and made me vitally aware of just who I was.

I said, 'You figure they'll ever find out who did it?'

'Want a straight answer?'

'Do you think I want you to lie to me?'

'No, I don't figure that.'

'So?'

'I don't suppose they'll ever find out who did it, Matt.'

'Will they try?'

'I don't think so.'

'Would you, if it were your case?'

He looked at me. 'Well, I'll be perfectly honest with you,' he said after a moment's thought. 'I don't know. I'd like to think I'd try. I think some – I think, *fuck* it, I think a couple of our own must of done it. What the hell else can you think, right?'

'Right.'

'Whoever did it was a fucking idiot. An absolute fucking idiot who just did the department more harm than Broadfield could ever hope to do. Whoever did it ought to hang by the neck, and I like to think I'd go after the bastards with everything I had if it was my case.' He lowered his eyes. 'But to be honest, I don't know if I would. I think I'd go through the motions and sweep it under the rug.'

'And that's what they'll do out in Queens.'

'I didn't talk to them. I don't know for a fact that's what they'll do. But I'd be surprised if they did anything else, and so would you.'

'Uh-huh.'

'What are you going to do, Matt.'

'Me?' I stared at him. 'Me? What *should* I do?'

'I mean, are you going to try and go after them? Because I don't know if it's a good idea.'

'Why should I do that, Eddie?' I spread my hands palms up. 'He's not my cousin. And nobody's hiring me to find out who killed him.'

'Is that straight?'

'It's straight.'

'You're hard to figure. I think I got you pegged, and then I don't.' He stood up and put some money on the table. 'Let me buy that round,' he said.

'Stick around, Eddie. Have another drink.'

He hadn't done more than touch the one he'd had. 'No time,' he said. 'Matt, you don't have to crawl into the bottle just because of this. It doesn't change anything.'

'It doesn't?'

'Hell, no. You still got a life of your own. You got this woman you're seeing, you got—'

'No.'

'Huh?'

'Maybe I'll see her again. I don't know. Probably not. She could have called by this time. And after it happened, you would think she'd have called if it was real.'

'I don't follow you.'

But I wasn't talking to him. 'We were in the right place at the right time,' I went on. 'So it looked as though we might turn out to be important for each other. If it ever had a chance, I'd say the chance died this morning when the gun went off.'

'Matt, you're not making sense.'

'It makes sense to me. Maybe that's my fault. We might see each other again, I don't know. But whether we do or don't, it's not going to change anything. People don't get to change things. Things change people once in a while, but people don't change things.'

'I gotta go, Matt. Take it a little easy on the booze, huh?'

'Sure, Eddie.'

Sometime that night I dialed her number in Forest Hills. The phone rang a dozen times before I gave up and got my dime back.

I called another number. A leftover voice recited, 'Seven-two-five-five. I am sorry, but no one is at home at the moment. If you will leave your name and number at the sound of the tone, your call will be returned as soon as possible. Thank you.'

The tone sounded, and it was my turn. But I couldn't seem to think of anything to say.